The Plays of Robert Munford

The First Comic Plays Written in America

The Patriots — The Candidates

With an introduction by

Robert A. Armour
Virginia Commonwealth University

Geodesics Publishing Inc.
848 N. Rainbow Blvd. #2269
Las Vegas, Nevada 89107
2008

These plays were first published under the title *A Collection of Plays and Poems, by the late Colonel Robert Munford, of Mecklenburg, in the State of Virginia*, by William Printis of Petersburg, Virginia, in 1798.

Cover artwork by Steve Warner.

Contents

INTRODUCTION

Colonial American Theater

During the lifetime of Robert Munford III, of Virginia, colonial theater developed from the crude amateur productions to more polished and widely popular professional performances. American theater remained derivative of English drama until after the Revolution, when Americans became more conscious of their nationality. Nevertheless, in the slightly more than one hundred years between the first American theatrical performance and the war for independence, Americans, especially those living in the larger cities, developed a taste for the theater.

During the colonial period, Virginia, where the Anglican Church did not seriously hamper theatrical activity on moral grounds, scored four firsts in the history of the American stage: the first performance, the first play written by an American, the first building built to serve as a theater, and America's first comic plays. It is this climate which nurtured the literary efforts of the man who is generally credited with being America's first comic dramatist.

On August 27, 1665, three gentlemen presented America's first play, *The Bare and the Cub* at Cowle's Tavern in Accomac County, on Virginia's Eastern Shore. A local citizen, offended by the immorality of acting, brought the men before the court. The justices of the court ordered the three to appear the next day fully costumed and prepared to demonstrate their play for the pleasure of the court. Apparently the judges liked what they saw, for they found the three not guilty of any fault and ordered the complaining citizen to pay all court costs.

However precedent setting, this play did not stimulate immediate imitation. Other theatrical productions were slow to develop, which is not too surprising since most Americans at the time were busy with matters of survival. Nevertheless in 1702 students at the College of William and Mary put on a play; and the following year Anthony Aston, an Englishman come to America, wrote and acted in plays in Charleston and New York. He is credited with being the first professional actor to work in the colonies.

The initial theater in the new land was built by William Levingston, a Scottish merchant, who began a dancing school in Williamsburg in 1716. Lessons at the school were taught by Charles Stagg and his wife Mary, who had both been indentured to Levingston the previous year. The Staggs apparently had knowledge of the theater, as well as dancing, and the couple and Levingston soon entered into an agreement to build and operate a theater. Levingston bought lots from the City of Williamsburg facing the Palace Green in November, 1716, and began construction. By the time the theater was completed in the spring of 1718, the Staggs had freed themselves of their indenture. They formed a small acting company, possibly filled out by other actors indentured to Levingston. Little is known of their productions since there was no newspaper in Williamsburg until 1736. Scant archeological evidence shows that the theater was approximately thirty feet wide and eighty-six and a half feet long. It was constructed of wood, but nothing is known of its interior. The building was used for local productions and for other entertainments through the years, but by the early 1740s it had fallen into disuse. In 1745 it was used for municipal purposes and converted into a courthouse.

In the 1730s there were tentative beginnings of theater in other colonies. In 1730 an amateur company in New York brought Shakespeare before an American audience for the first time. Two years later a professional company acted a series of English plays for New Yorkers, but performances there were to remain irregular for the next two decades. In Charleston, South Carolina, however, theater took a firmer hold. Using a courtroom for a theater, a company of actors began a theatrical season of English plays in the winter of 1735. The next year Charlestonians welcomed the opening of a new theater and its first production— George Farquhar's comedy, *The Recruiting Officer*. By spring of 1737, however, the fortunes of this facility had declined and it closed.

In 1749 a company of actors organized under the management of Walter Murray and Thomas Kean, and they raised the quality of American theater a notch. Beginning in Philadelphia, they soon moved to New York, where they remained in residence until the summer of 1751. They then removed to Williamsburg, where Alexander Finnie, proprietor of the Raleigh Tavern built them a theater. They opened in their new home in October with *Richard III* and continued their season into November. They returned to the city the following April, after a short time in Petersburg, putting on Farquhar's new play, *The Constant Couple, or a Trip to the Jubilee*. Closing in Williamsburg, this time for good, they traveled northward to Tappahannock, Fredericksburg (where George Washington apparently saw his first play) and onward into Maryland. They left behind in the Virginia capital a reputation for "loose behavior" and some agitation among local citizens for legislation against actors, which fortunately never came to effect. Few of these actors were fully professional; and when times became hard, they disbanded and returned to prior trades.

In the meantime, the first truly professional company of actors had arrived from London with new sets and new plays, an event which marked the beginning of professional theater in America. Lewis Hallam's Company of Comedians moved into the renovated theater vacated by the Murray-Kean company and produced its first evening's bill on September 15, 1752. The play was *The Merchant of Venice*, followed by a farce. During the spring and fall the actors presented plays three times a week. Likely the presentations included more Shakespeare, William Congreve's *Love for Love*, George Farquhar's *The Beaux' Stratagem*, Richard Steele's *The Conscious Lovers*, Joseph Addison's *The Drummer*, and Colley Cibber's *The Careless Husband*. It is recorded that on November 9, 1752, Governor Robert Dinwiddie entertained the chief of the Cherokee nation, his wife and warriors at a performance of *Othello*, perhaps chosen because American Indians were sometimes then called Moors. The company left Williamsburg and went on for seasons in New York, Philadelphia, and Annapolis before returning to Williamsburg in 1760 under the new management of David Douglass. George Washington's account book shows that he bought tickets in October that year while he was in town for the session of the House of Burgesses.

When Douglass left for other markets, one of his actors—William Verling—formed his own troupe, which he called the Virginia Company of Comedians. Verling was known as one of the finest actors of his day; and his female lead, Henrietta Osborne, captured many a heart with both her talent and her beauty. Both Washington and Thomas Jefferson record frequent purchases of tickets and refreshments at the theater. Plays included the usual comedies, farces, and John Gay's *The Beggar's Opera*, and they were performed in other Virginia cities, such as Norfolk and Alexandria, as well as in Williamsburg.

In June, 1770, Douglass returned his company—now called the American Company—to Williamsburg. His star was Nancy Hallam whose acting and personal beauty and charm also attracted a sizable following among the men of the city. Washington and Jefferson were again frequently in the audience, along with many others who found in the theater one of the chief social activities Williamsburg had to offer.

In April, 1772, Douglass left Williamsburg, and the theater closed until after the war. The company toured other cities until 1774, when the Continental Congress passed an edict which called on American citizens to refrain from diversions and entertainments, including plays, because of the pending troubles with the mother country. The climate was not good for English actors and English plays, and American theater—so heavily dependent on them—effectively shut itself down until after the war.

While there is no proof that Robert Munford attended the theater in Williamsburg, the supposition is strong that he did. Theatrical companies timed their presence in Williamsburg for court and legislative sessions, and records show that other Virginia politicians frequently attended the plays. Since the theater in the decade before the war was a major source of social activity, it is likely that Munford joined his fellow legislators for performances. This is the theatrical milieu, then, which produced the first comedies written on this side of the Atlantic.

Robert Munford

In 1798 William Printis, from Petersburg, Virginia, printed a thin volume of plays and poetry by Robert Munford. One of the largest planters and landholders in southern Virginia, Munford was a colonel in the revolutionary army and delegate to the legislature in Williamsburg. Literature for him was an avocation; but he produced two plays and several poems that still please. As, probably, the first American to write comic plays, he has a place in literary history, but his greatest contribution today is his description of various aspects of colonial life, such as elections and the issue of patriotism during the Revolutionary War, which are infrequently portrayed in the literature of the day.

Colonel Munford had been dead for fifteen years when his plays and poems were edited for publication by his son, William, himself a poet. He tells us he wanted to preserve the memory of his father and to offer amusement to those who might read the works. William Munford wrote in his preface to the volume, "The author appears to have thoroughly understood the true points of ridicule in human characters, and to have drawn them with great accuracy and variety in his comedies." There is also some evidence that William was preparing the plays for a stage production.

Life

Robert Munford, the dramatist, was the third in a line of Robert Munfords. The family had not been especially distinguished in the seventeenth century, but the first Robert, the dramatist's grandfather, began to accumulate land and prestige early in the eighteenth century. Overseer, attorney, and friend to William Byrd II, Munford became socially and politically prominent on the Southside (that part of Virginia south of the

James River, west of the coastal region, and east of the foothills of the Blue Ridge Mountains). Munford, vestryman of Bristol Parish and churchwarden, was elected to represent Prince George County in the House of Burgesses. He died in 1735.

Robert Munford II inherited his father's estate and William Byrd's influence. He personally added to his position by marrying Anna Bland, whose family gave him relationships to the Lees, Beverlys, Byrds, and Randolphs, as well as the Blands—all among the most prominent families of eighteenth-century Virginia. Like his father, Robert II served in the vestry and the House of Burgesses, but he was less fortunate than the first Robert. He lost money and had to mortgage his home, Whitehall. After his death about 1745, his widow had to sell off a good portion of the estate to pay his debts.

Robert III, the dramatist, was born probably in 1737 and was about eight when his father died. He went to live at Blandfield, the home of his uncle, William Beverley, in Essex County, Virginia, along the south banks of the Rappahannock River. When he was about fourteen, Robert's uncle took him and his cousin to England for schooling. Under Master John Clarke, first at Beverley School, then at Wakefield Grammar School, the boys received a classical education and were probably exposed to classical drama. At his uncle's death in 1756, Robert returned to Virginia to meet a new stepfather and new half sisters and to go to Williamsburg to study law under the guidance of the King's Attorney, Peyton Randolph.

Munford's study was interrupted when he left Williamsburg to serve under William Byrd III and George Washington in the French and Indian War. As an result of his recruiting ability, he was appointed lieutenant and later captain. He wrote to his Uncle Bland of the life in camps—of the waiting to fight, of his respect for Col. Washington, of the smallpox and the flux, of the lice. But the Virginians saw little action, and Munford returned to Williamsburg to finish his study.

By 1760 his legal preparation was complete, and he went to Lunenburg County to supervise the land and slaves he had inherited. During the next five years he was to create a comfortable position for himself as husband, planter, and politician. In 1761 he married his cousin Anna Beverley; and with her dowry and other resources he began adding acres and slaves to his estate, becoming one of the largest landholders in the area. As a planter, his cash crop was tobacco, but his farms also produced the household necessities: corn; cattle for milk, butter, and meat; sheep for wool and mutton; and hogs. In 1765 he began to build his home, Richland—a spacious two story white frame building with wings.

Politics, however, were to take much of his time from his family and plantation. Wou'dbe in *The Candidates* expressed the attitude of many of the Virginia aristocracy toward public service when he addressed a reluctant candidate for public office: "I believe you enjoy as much domestic happiness as any person, and that your aversion to a public life proceeds from the pleasure you find at home. But sir, it surely is the duty of every man who has abilities to serve his country, to take up the burden, and bear it with patience." When the southern part of Lunenburg County split off and became Mecklenburg County in 1764, Munford was asked to take up the burden. He was first appointed Session Magistrate, then County Lieutenant responsible for the militia, and later treasurer for the county. In 1765 he followed the steps of his grandfather and father to the House of Burgesses in Williamsburg. In five years he had risen to a position of prominence and influence in county affairs, but now he was to go to the capital and take his place in the affairs of the colony that were to lead to the Revolution.

His first few years as a member of the House were uneventful. Frequently the House met only briefly to take care of local matters, and Munford devoted most of his time to his suffering financial affairs. War sentiments did not run strong in Virginia in the early 1770s, but by 1775 American nationalism was growing. As a young man in the House of Burgesses, Munford had aligned himself with Patrick Henry and other liberals, but his own financial problems seem to have made him reluctant to sever commercial ties with England. The decision of loyalty must have caused him pain; but in April, 1775, Munford wrote to William Byrd III, himself a loyalist, that he believed civil war was inevitable but that he would make one more effort to preserve "civil order" through an appeal to both John Murray, Earl of Dunmore, the governor, and the more radical colonists for moderation.

This position in the middle could not hold. The governor forced the Burgesses to become aggressive, and Munford accepted a leadership role in the political maneuvering, serving that spring on nine of the fifteen committees that represented the House in its disputes with the governor.

On adjournment of the House of Burgesses in 1775 Munford returned home, where, despite his considerations for his relations with England, he was asked to remain as County Lieutenant. As such, he was responsible for recruiting for the regular army and for preparing the local militia.

By 1779 his service had completely restored the voters' faith in his loyalty, and he was elected to serve in the first session of the House of Delegates where he was to be highly respected. The confidence his colleagues had in him is reflected by the committees on which he was asked to serve, joining Thomas Jefferson, Patrick Henry, John Tyler, and George Mason as among the most active delegates. His most important work concerned the organization of the Virginia Militia.

Despite early success, the Virginia troops met disasters in 1780, and evidently Munford was held partly responsible for defeats at Charleston and Camden, South Carolina. When he returned to the House in October, 1780, he was not given his usual appointments to important committees and instead was assigned routine duties. For some reason, perhaps his cool reception in the House, or perhaps his need to give attention to the military situation in Mecklenburg County, he shortly left his post in Williamsburg and returned home to his duties as County Lieutenant and quartermaster.

With the title of colonel, Munford led his troops southward into North Carolina at the threat of invasion from British troops moving northward. Despite an severe attack of the gout, Col. Munford was in command of his troops when they engaged the enemy at Guildford Court House, March, 1781. This time the Virginia troops distinguished themselves; and with some satisfaction, Munford returned home to recover from his illness. His career as a soldier was over, but he continued to act as quartermaster for some time.

The last two years of his life saw the decline of his capabilities, probably as a result of increasing illness and drink. He resigned his positions as County Lieutenant and Magistrate, and spent his last days uncomfortably at home. His death came apparently just before the end of the year 1783.

His Poetry

The 1798 edition of the plays also included a number of poems of varying merit. Several of the poems use good humor, lively narrative, and contemporary satire. One poem is a translation of the first book of Ovid's *Metamorphoses* in heroic couplets. Perhaps his best poetic work is *The Ram: A Tale*—a mock heroic epic satirizing fashions of women's hair styles. The poem owes much to Samuel Butler and Alexander Pope. Three more poems create satiric correspondence between the devil and his earth-bound son. The devil takes pride in his corrupt son, but is concerned he might be turning good. The son replies that what in him seems good is only hypocrisy. A few other less interesting poems complete the collection.

The final poem, *A Patriotic Song*, is a nationalistic drinking song, a version of which appears satirically in *The Patriots*. It should put to rest any lingering doubts about Munford's loyalty to the American cause during the Revolutionary War:

> Come on, my brave fellows, a fig for our lives.
>> We'll fight for our country, our children and wives.
> Determin'd we are to live happy and free;
>> Then join honest fellows in chorus with me.
>>> Derry down, down, &c.

We'll drink our own liquor, our brandy from peaches,
   A fig for the English, they may kiss all our breeches.
Those blood-sucking, beer-drinking puppies retreat;
   But our peach-brandy fellows can never be beat.
      Derry down, down, &c.

A fig for the English, and Hessians to boot,
   Who are sick half their time with eating of crout,
But bacon and greens, and Indian corn-bread,
   Make a buck-skin jump up, tho' he seem to be dead,
      Derry down, down, &c.

His Drama

The Candidates is set in Virginia during the election that followed the death of Norbonne Berkeley, Baron de Botetourt, one of Virginia's most popular royal governors, on October 1, 1770. Therefore, it was most likely not written earlier than the following winter. *The Patriots* makes references to events that took place in the spring of 1777, and therefore must date later than those months. Most likely both plays were written before 1780 as Munford was both busy and ill the last years of his life. This would generally date both plays in the 1770s. In 1787 Royal Tyler's *The Contrast* became the first comedy written by an American to be produced on the stage. That Munford wrote his plays before Tyler wrote *The Contrast* is a certainty. Like Tyler, Munford probably wrote his plays to be produced, but there is no evidence that they ever were during his life time.

The plays analyze problems that transcend the eighteenth century. *The Candidates* is concerned with one's obligation to serve his country and with the necessity for selecting the proper persons to serve in the government. It also deals with other contemporary issues, such as political corruption, unfair campaign practices, and unpopular taxes. *The Patriots* raises the question of the nature of true loyalty to one's country. The contemporaneity of this play is demonstrated by the fact that in 1971, at the height of the controversy over the obligation of citizens to support their country's action in Viet Nam, it was produced in New York at a Greenwich Village theatre.

As Munford was educated in England and continued business interests there, it is no surprise that his plays are a blend of the English and the American. The traditions of the English theater, as represented by writers like Farquhar and Susanah Centlivre, were well known to him. He had seen plays while a schoolboy in England, and he undoubtedly read English plays in his library. He must have witnessed some of the English plays produced in Williamsburg. The influence of this English tradition on Munford's play is seen, for example, in his choice of genres (farce and comedy) and of techniques and conventions (slapstick, repartee, comic servants, etc.).

Munford, however, was no slave to his English sources. The American characteristics of the plays are deeper than simply setting them in America. He invigorated some of characters with distinctly American traits, such as permitting some characters to exhibit the sometime Virginia propensity for both alcohol and horse racing. But more important are the American political system that is the basis for *The Candidates* and the American point of view during the war in *The Patriots*. In these plays Munford has, in fact, given us a rare glimpse into two areas of colonial life rarely depicted in the literature of the day: the election of the political leaders who created this country and the pain of choosing sides during the Revolutionary War.

The Candidates

The strengths of *The Candidates* lie in its realism, its political commentary, and above all its humor. There is no question that the dramatic form of the play is derivative; it is a farce which combines humor with serious comments. The plot is simple: several men are running for the House of Burgesses in colonial Virginia, and we are witness to the campaign and election. The characters are typed and shallow.

Munford has found humor in all aspects of Virginia life. He begins by allowing Sir John Toddy, Munford's unworthy candidate for office, to get caught in a contradiction. Munford's hero, Wou'dbe, suspecting that Sir John has come to ask his support in the election, bluntly asks whether the purpose of Sir John's call is political: "No, sir, upon my honour, sir, it was punctually to know how your lady and family did, Sir, 'pon honour, sir, it was." But a few lines later when Sir John becomes flustered on discovering that Wou'dbe himself intends to run, he admits the truth, "My business, sir, was to get the favor of you to speak a good word for me among the people." Hypocrisy is one of the chief objects of satire in this period. Much of Munford's humor results from the candidates revealing the shallowness of his characters' thinking, the preposterousness of their political ambition, and the self-aggrandizement of their actions.

The common citizens are probably Munford's best source of humor. Their drinking, their fighting, their discussing the candidates all provide laughter, but Munford also shows them to be people of good sense when it is necessary. Both Guzzle and his wife, for example, are renowned for their drinking ability, but poor Joan drinks more than she should and passes out. Her husband and friends place her limp body next to the equally drunk Sir John in order to watch their reactions when they come to. On awaking, she is sure she has done something to make her husband jealous and begins beating Sir John, the cause, she thinks, of her misbehavior: "I'll learn you," she cries, "to cuckold a man without letting his wife know it." The shrewish wife has been a source of comedy for centuries, but Munford has used the old device well.

The scene in which the women argue politics with their husbands is one of the most entertaining in the play:

> *Lucy.*   If the wives were to vote, I believe they would make a better
>   choice than their husbands.
> *Twist.*   You'd be for the funnyest—wou'dn't you?
> *Lucy.*   Yes, faith; and the wittiest, and the prettiest, and the wisest, and
>   the best too; you are all for ugly except when you choose
>   me.

Ralpho, Wou'dbe's man servant, is supposed to be a comic figure; but while he does cause a few smiles today, he is not overly successful as a comic. The relationship between master and saucy servant is old subject matter for literature, and Munford has done little to improve on his sources. Ralpho begs a new suit of clothes so that he can impress the girls. He tries to imitate his master's command of the language but the results are malaprophisisms ("This figure of mine is not reconsiderable in its delurement and when I'm dressed out like a gentleman, the girls I'm a thinking, will find me disistible."). He is a coward and runs from a woman when she attacks him. He lies, or at least stretches the truth, when he thinks the truth will get him in trouble. For example, he had been ordered to take care of the drunk Sir John, but when Joan goes into her rage in the scene mentioned above, he runs off leaving Sir John at her mercy. Later when questioned by Wou'dbe about Sir John's whereabouts, he gives an imaginative answer:

> *Wou'dbe.* Where's Sir John??
> *Ralpho.* In the hands of a woman, sir, and as I left him in such good
>   hands, I thought there was no farther occasion for my atten-
>   dance.
> *Wou'dbe.* Are you sure he'll be taken care of?
> *Ralpho.* Yes, the lady, an't please your honour, seemed devilish kind
>   to him.

Munford's humor blends into his satire with ease. The prologue to the play was written by "A Friend"—many suspect William Munford— but it clearly identifies drunkenness and monarchy as the objects of the satire:

The state of things was such, in former times,
'Ere wicked kings were punished'd for their crimes;
Then strove the candidates to gain their feats
Most heartily, with drinking bouts, and treats;
The meanest vices all the people stain'd,
And drunkenness, and monarchy both reign'd,
With such strong cause his anger to engage,
How could our Bard restrain satiric rage?
But, God forbid, its edge shou'd now apply,
Or on our race-field, when you cast an eye
You there a home-election—should espy.
Science and virtue, now are wider spread,
And crown with dignity, fair Freedom's head.
We only pray this satire ne'er be just,
Save when apply'd to other times, and trust.
Its keenness only, a rememb-rancer,
And guard from future evils, may appear.

The purpose, then, of the satire is to "guard from future evils," to see that the vices exposed in the satire do not continue to infest the country. William Munford acknowledged the same purpose in the prose preface to his edition of the plays: "The piece entitled, *The Candidates,* is intended to laugh to scorn the practice of corruption, and falsehood; of which too many are guilty in electioneering; to teach our countrymen to despise the arts of those who meanly attempt to influence their votes by anything but merit."

Since he is writing farce, Munford's major satiric device is exaggeration. Following age-old satiric conventions, Munford uses the names of his characters to indicate their traits he intends to ridicule through exaggeration. Sir John Toddy, John Guzzle and Joan Guzzle have a fondness for drink. Strutabout is vain—vain enough to think he will be the people's choice; Smallhopes makes noise like a candidate even though he has no chance of being elected.

The realism of the play serves to keep it from being reduced to a slapstick burlesque without serious purpose. Munford's own involvement in politics would suggest to us that he took politics seriously and that he was careful to describe the election accurately.

The gentry felt an obligation to run for public office; as noted earlier, Wou'dbe impressed on Worthy the obligation he had to serve his country. These men were reluctant to give up the comforts of their home life to "take up the burden." Worthy says, "I have little inclination to the service; you know my aversion to public life"; and Wou'dbe himself is reluctant to stand for office, "Must I again be subject to the humors of a fickle crowd? Must I again resign my reason, and be nought but what each voter pleases? Must I cajole, fawn, and wheedle, for a place that brings so little profit?"

Other less suitable members of the gentry felt less hesitation to offer themselves for election, and so the election fight was on. Sir John, Strutabout, and Smallhopes used irregular methods to win votes—bribes, fights, liquor, lies; and it was up to the freeholders, the common people, to determine which of the gentry deserved to serve. Munford must have had a high opinion of these people because he put much trust in their ability to choose justly. The people debate the candidates' merits and accept their drink and food; but when it comes time to vote, they vote their conscience. Twist says, "Some of them [the candidates] had better keep their money; I'll vote for no man but to my liking."

Worthy and Wou'dbe campaign also, but in a refined manner. Wou'dbe will buy a man a drink and invites many fellow citizens to a shad breakfast, but both are reluctant to ask for votes for themselves. They simply answer questions honestly and only promise to do what they can. The citizens recognize men of quality and Worthy and Wou'dbe are duly elected. Even drunken Sir John supports them in the end: "Huzza for Mr. Worthy and Mr. Wou'dbe!" I'm not so fitten as they, and therefore gentlemen I recline. Yes, gentlemen, I will; for I'm not so fitten as they."

It would appear that Munford's faith in the freeholders to elect the proper people was based on reality, and this play may well help to explain how the Virginia system of democracy was able to produce such political leaders as Jefferson, Washington, Madison, Lee, and Munford. These men accepted their duty to serve, and the freeholders had the good sense to recognize their abilities.

The Patriots

The Patriots is more ambitious and more finished than *The Candidates.* It is not farce but a well-developed comedy. The fullness of the play is the result of a multiplicity of plots; Munford presents his audience with three love plots and a loyalty plot, all of which are rather skillfully interwoven. The use of several plots is, of course, common in sentimental comedy, as are some of Munford's other theatrical conventions, such as concealed identity, farcical marriages, and reformed scoundrels. These devices are typical of sentimental comedy, but Munford has given them some fresh touches, like regional dialects for the Virginians and the Scotsmen.

The genre of the play is that of the sentimental comedy, but Munford has serious points to make about love, marriage and war. The satire is largely parody, which would have been better recognized by Munford's contemporaries familiar with the people of Mecklenburg County, as the playwright seems to have used the occasion of the play to score points on a few of the leaders of Southside society. The parody, however, is broad and does include an attack on falsely used sentiment that gives a more universal character to the satire. The farce is well done and humorous, especially in the marriage scene in which the reluctant butler-cum-preacher pretends to be unable to read in order to delay the ruin of the innocent Melinda. The irony is a bit obvious: Men who claim loyalty are really cowards, men who are quiet are really the most loyal Americans, poor servants are really wealthy, etc.

The use of sentimentalism places this play firmly in the convention of eighteenth-century English literature, but Munford on his own, has apparently distinguished three uses of overindulgent sentiment—two of which he disapproves, one he seems to like. Isabella—a female politician, as Munford describes her—represents the serious use of overstated senti-ment; she believes what she says, but her sentiments are so "exalted" they bear little resemblance to reality:

Isabella. Lord, no, but then there's something so clever in fighting and dying for one's country; and the officers look so clever and smart; I declare I never saw an ugly officer in my life.

Mira. Your fancy must be a great beautifier, as many of them are not much indebted to nature for personal charms.

Isabella. Ay, that's because you are not in love with an officer. When you are, you'll think as I do.

Mira. Are you in love with one?

Isabella. Ah! Now that's an ill-natured question, I tell you, child,I am in love with nothing but my country. If, indeed, a man should approach me, who would lay his laurels at my feet, who could count his glorious scars gained in the front of victory, I might look upon him.

Mira. I suppose, then, if he wanted an arm, or leg or an eye, it would be all the better; or a great cut over his eye-brow would be a beauty spot.

Isabella. Certainly. Nothing can be more elegant. It appears so mar-tial—so—so—quite the thing.

Mira. Well! I'm afraid my taste will never be quite so grand as your's, tho' I hope I love my country as well as you.

Isabella. You love your country! Your sentiments are not refined enough; they are not exalted to the level of patriotism; for my part, I scorn to think of anything else.

Flash is also guilty of this sort of sentimentalism: "Fighting! 'Tis victuals and drink to me. I could breakfast upon fighting, dine and sup upon fighting. . . ."

The problem with Isabella and Flash's use of sentiment is that they believe their romantic notions of love and war. Pickle represents a differ-ent type of sentiment. He uses a similar exalted sentiment but he recognizes its falseness and uses it only for personal gain. Despicable and hypocritical, but at least he is honest with himself:

> Ha, a beautiful creature, by my soul! artless and inocent no doubt. (I'll try my luck with her by God) let me see (musing) I'll take her in the old way, I believe: address her in heroics, talk of my honourable intentions, and promise marriage. Come to my assistance, dear cunning, and sweet dissimulation; ye true harbingers of lust and love.

He gives poor Melinda his concocted line, "If I marry a poor girl, I get a wife; if a rich one, I get a mistress." And she falls, but ironically not for his sentiment but because he calls her "miss" and seems to be a member of the gentry who treats a country girl with respect.

Mira apparently represents Munford's attitude toward sentiment. First she recognizes false sentiment in others. When Flash boasts of his military ability but then says he could quit the army for Mira, she replies, tongue in-cheek, "For shame, sir, what! desert the service of your country, when she most stands in need of your assistance." But she can use true sentiment, sentiment that is genuinely felt and realistic enough to be feasible. She tells her father, "My principal study, sir, is to please my father," and she means it when she says it, even though she later decides to run away with Trueman against her father's wishes. Additionally she is not devoid of sentiment when it comes to love or war, but it is properly restrained: "I acknowledge the smiles of beauty should reward the man who bravely asserts his country's rights, and meets her enemies in the bloody field . . . ."

The serious theme of the play is political loyalty, but Munford resolves its conflict in the fourth act and devotes the rest of the play to the love plot. Nevertheless, the issue of loyalty is the one Munford wanted to emphasize and the sentimental comedy was a vehicle for his more serious theme. Munford himself had felt the sting of gossip of disloyalty; and even though this play has a well constructed light touch, the play seems to be his answer to his critics.

The theme is brought into focus by the Committee of Observation, which had responsibility for discovering those still loyal to the crown. Those suspected of disloyalty to the American cause were first asked to take an oath of allegiance. If they refused, they were coerced to renounce their misguided ways. If they persisted in their error, they were disarmed or banished. In *The Patriots* the Committee tries three Scotsmen for loyalty, and the trial and the discussion that surrounds it give Munford an opportunity to define loyalty. Tackabout illustrates the type of popular loyalty that is all empty air:

> Where is the man that has done more than I have? I have damn'd the ministry' abus'd the king, vilified the parliament, and curs'd the Scotch.

I have raised the people's suspicions against all moderate men; advised them to spurn at all government: I have cried down tories, cried up whigs, extolled Washington as a god, and call'd Howe a very devil. I have exclaimed against all taxes, advised the people to pay no debts; I have promised them success in war, a free trade, and independent dominion. In short, I have inspired them with the true patriotic fire, the spirit of opposition; and yet you say it is expected I should do something.

Munford's hero, Meanwell, exposes the emptiness of Tackabout's boasts and expresses the type of loyalty that was to inspire the Americans during the war:

Men who aim at power without merit, must conceal the meanness of their souls by noisy and passionate speeches in favour of every thing which is the current opinion of the day; but real patriots are mild, and secretly anxious for their country, but modest in expressions of zeal. They are industrious in the public service, but claim no glory to themselves.

Elsewhere Meanwell has said, "I hope my zeal against tyranny will not be skewn by bowling against it, but by serving my country against her enemies."

Munford's satiric attack against false loyalty is most pronounced in the trial scenes. In the first, the Scotsmen are tried not on evidence of disloyalty but simply because they are Scotsmen. The ridiculousness is heightened by McFlint who quickly denied his motherland and is found innocent by his jurors on his word that he was not born in Scotland. A second trial scene (not officially a trial) occurs when Meanwell and Trueman are confronted by the committee. Trueman frustrates their charges by showing the shallowness of their thinking:

Trueman. Explain what you mean by the word tory, gentlemen.
Simple.   Tory! Why surely everybody knows what a tory is—a tory is.
             Pray, gentlemen, explain to him what a tory is.
Strut.   A tory, sir, is any one who disapproves of men and measures.
Brazen.   All suspected persons are called tories.
Trueman. If suspicion makes a tory, I may be one; if a disapprobation
             of men and measures constitutes a tory, I am one; but if a
             real attachment to the true interests of my country stamps
             me her friend, then I detest the opprobrious epithet of tory,
             as much as I do the inflammatory distinction of whig.

The humor, satire, descriptions of important events in eighteenth-century life, and social issues which remain important today, make Robert Munford a man of his time and a writer for ours. As most likely America's first comic dramatist, he has a place in American theatrical history. More importantly, as a writer who caught some of the humor of life, who satirized the foibles of humans, who addressed significant topics such as patriotism and duty, he remains a playwright we should read and remember.

A Note on the Text

This edition of the plays has been taken primarily from a copy of the 1798 edition owned by the late Mr. Beverley Bland Munford, Jr. of Richmond, Virginia. I am most grateful to Mr. Munford and his family for allowing me to reproduce his copy. Editions in the Virginia State Library and the Virginia Historical Society were also consulted.

It should be noted that the playwright did not have the opportunity to correct his plays in galley proofs. As the 1798 edition was carelessly printed and edited, I have made whatever textual corrections are necessary to allow the modern reader to read with ease. I have modernized the long s, regularized capitalization, changed punctuation where the original misled, and corrected obvious typographical errors.

Bibliography

Baine, Rodney M. *Robert Munford: America's First Comic Dramatist.* Athens: The University of Georgia Press, 1967.

Canby, Courtlandt, ed., "Robert Munford's The Patriots," *William and Mary Quarterly,* 3rd series VI (July, 1949), pp. 437-502.

Carson, Jane. *Colonial Virginians at Play.* Williamsburg, VA: The Colonial Williamsburg Foundation, 1989.

Hubbell, Jay B. *The South in American Literature.* Durham: Duke University Press, 1954.

——— and Douglass Adair, eds., "The Candidates; or, The Humours of a Virginia Election," *William and Mary Quarterly,* 3rd. series V (April, 1948), pp. 217-57.

McNamara, Brooks. *The American Playhouse in the Eighteenth Century.* Cambridge, MA: Harvard University Press, 1969.

Munford, Robert. *A Collection of Plays and Poems, by the late Colonel Robert Munford, of Mecklenburg, in the State of Virginia.* Petersburg,VA,: William Printis, 1798.

Quinn, Arthur Hobson. *A History of the American Drama from the Beginning to the Civil War.* New York: Appleton-Century-Crofts, 1923, 1951.

Rankin, Hugh F. *The Theater in Colonial America.* Chapel Hill: The University of North Carolina Press, 1965.

Vaughn, Jack A. *Early American Dramatists from the Beginnings to 1900.* New York: Frederick Ungar Publishing Co., 1981.

Young, William C. *Documents of American Theater History: Famous American Playhouses, 1716-1899.* Vol. I. Chicago: American Library Association, 1973.

THE CANDIDATES

- OR -

THE
HUMORS OF A VIRGINIA
ELECTION.

A COMEDY

IN THREE ACTS.

DRAMATIS PERSONAE.

Sir John Toddy,
Mr. Wou'dbe,
Mr. Strutabout,
Mr. Smallhopes,

Candidates for the office of delegates to the general assembly.

Mr. Julip,
Capt. Paunch,

Gentlemen Justices.

Mr. Worthy,

formerly a delegate, but now declines.

Guzzle,
Twist,
Stern,
Prize,

Freeholders.

Ralpho,

Wou'dbe's servant.

Jack,

a tool to Mr. Strutabout.

Ned,

the same to Mr. Smallhopes.

Mrs. Guzzle,
Lucy Twist,
Catharine Stern,
Sarah Prize,

Freeholders' wives

Freeholders, Country girls, &c.

PROLOGUE

BY A FRIEND.

LADIES and gentlemen, to-night you'll see
A bard delighting in satiric glee;
In merry scenes his biting tale unfold,
And high to Folly's eye the mirror hold:
Here eager candidates shall call for votes,
And bawling voters louder stretch their throats:
Here may you view, in groups diverting, join'd
The poor and wealthy rabble of mankind;
All who deserve the lash, the lash will find.
Here characters, whose names are now unknown,
Shall shine again, as in their spheres they shone;
While some may make malicious explanation,
And know them all still living in the nation.
If any present, say, fie, shameless bard!
Hast thou for decency no more regard
Than at thy betters, thus to make a stand,
And boldly point out meanness, contraband,
Depreciating the wisdom of the land?
Tho' such, the wond'rous sympathy of wits,
That every fool will wear the cap that fits,
I boldly answer, how could he mean you,
Who, when he wrote, about you nothing knew?
The state of things was such, in former times,
'Ere wicked kings were punish'd for their crimes;
Then strove the candidates to gain their seats
Most heartily, with drinking bouts, and treats;
The meanest vices all the people stain'd,
And drunkenness, and monarchy both reign'd,
With such strong cause his anger to engage,
How could our Bard restrain satiric rage?
But, God forbid, its edge shou'd now apply,
Or on our race-field, when you cast an eye
You there a home-election—should espy.

Science and virtue, now are wider spread,
And crown with dignity, fair Freedom's head.
We only pray this satire ne'er be just,
Save when apply'd to other times, and trust
Its keenness only, a rememb'rancer,
And guard from future evils, may appear.
If, after this, objections should remain,
The motive's envy, consciousness disdain,
Or any thing, except the poet's want
Of sense, which no true publisher will grant.
Yet virtue is not in our story lost,
E'en then, Virginians could much virtue boast.
With plaudits, therefore, and free laughter own
Virginia's first and only comic son;
Ah! could the bard, rejoicing, raise his head
To hear his praise!—Alas! the bard is dead.

THE CANDIDATES.

ACT I. SCENE I.

Mr. Wou'dbe's house.

Enter Wol'dbe with a news-paper in his hand.

Wou'dbe. I am very sorry our good old governor Botetourt[1] has left us.
He well deserved our friendship, when alive, and that we
should for years to come, with gratitude, remember his mild
and affable deportment. Well, our little world will soon be up,
and very busy towards our next election. Must I again be subject to the humours of a fickle croud? Must I again resign my
reason, and be nought but what each voter pleases? Must I cajole, fawn, and wheedle, for a place that brings so little profit?

Enter Ralpho.

Ralpho. Sir John Toddy is below, and if your honour is at leisure, would
beg to speak to you.
Wou'dbe. My compliments to Sir John, and tell him, I shall be glad of
his company. So—Sir John, some time ago, heard me say I
was willing to resign my seat in the house to an abler person,
and he comes modestly to accept of it.

Enter Sir John Toddy.

Sir John. Mr. Wou'dbe, your most obedient servant, sir; I am proud to
find you well. I hope you are in good health, sir?
Wou'dbe. Very well, I am obliged to you, Sir John. Why, Sir John, you
surely are practising the grimace and compliments you intend
to make use of among the freeholders in the next election, and
have introduced yourself to me with the self-same common-
place expressions that we candidates adopt when we intend to

1 Norborne Berkeley, Baron de Botetourt, popular governor of Virginia, 1768-1770.

wheedle a fellow out of his vote—I hope you have no scheme upon me, Sir John?

Sir John. No, sir, upon my honour, sir, it was punctually to know how your lady and family did, sir; 'pon honour, sir, it was.

Wou'dbe. You had better be more sparing of your honour at present, Sir John; for, if you are a candidate, whenever you make promises to the people that you can't comply with, you must say "upon honour," otherwise they won't believe you.

Sir John. Upon honour, sir, I have no thought to set up for a candidate, unless you say the word.

Wou'dbe. Such condescension from you, Sir John, I have no reason to expect: you have my hearty consent to do as you please, and if the people choose you their Representative, I must accept of you as a colleague.

Sir John. As a colleague, Mr. Wou'dbe! I was thinking you did not intend to stand a poll, and my business, sir, was to get the favour of you to speak a good word for me among the people.

Wou'dbe. I hope you have no occasion for a trumpeter, Sir John? If you have, I'll speak a good word to you, and advise you to decline.

Sir John. Why, Mr. Wou'dbe, after you declin'd, I thought I was the next fittenest man in the county, and Mr. Wou'dbe, if you would be ungenerous, tho' you are a laughing man, you would tell me so.

Wou'dbe. It would be ungenerous indeed, Sir John, to tell you what the people could never be induced to believe. But I'll be ingenuous enough to tell you, Sir John, if you expect any assistance from me, you'll be disappointed, for I can't think you the *fittenest* man I know.

Sir John. Pray, sir, who do you know besides? Perhaps I may be thought as fit as your honour. But, sir, if you are for that, the hardest fend off: damn me, if I care a farthing for you; and so, your servant, sir. [*Exit Sir John.*

Wou'dbe. So, I have got the old knight, and his friend Guzzle, I suppose, against me, by speaking so freely; but their interest, I believe, has not weight enough among the people, for me to lose any thing, by making them my enemies. Indeed, the being intimate with such a fool as Sir John, might tend more to my discredit with them, for the people of Virginia have too much sense not to perceive how weak the head must be that is always filled with liquor. Ralpho!—

Enter Ralpho

Ralpho. Sir, what does your honour desire?

Wou'dbe. I'm going into my library, and if any gentleman calls, you may introduce him to me there.

Ralpho. Yes, sir. But, master, as election-times are coming, I wish you would remember a poor servant, a little.

Wou'dbe. What do you want?

Ralpho. Why, the last suit of clothes your honour gave me is quite worn out. Look here, *(shewing his elbows)* the insigns, (as I have heard your honour say, in one of your fine speeches) the insigns of faithful service. Now, methinks, as they that set up for burgesses, cut a dash, and have rare sport, why might not their servants have a little decreation?

Wou'dbe. I understand you, Ralpho, you wish to amuse yourself, and make a figure among the girls this election, and since such a desire is natural to the young and innocent if not carried to excess, I am willing to satisfy you; you may, therefore, have the suit I pulled off yesterday, and accept this present as an evidence that I am pleased with your diligence and fidelity, and am ever ready to reward it.   [*Exit Wou'dbe.*

Ralpho. God bless your honour! What a good master! Who would not do every thing to give such a one pleasure? But, e'gad, it's time to think of my new clothes: I'll go and try them on. Gadso! this figure of mine is not reconsiderable in its delurements, and when I'm dressed out like a gentleman, the girls, I'm a thinking, will find me desistible.   [*Exit.*

SCENE II.

A porch of a tavern: a Court-house on one side, and an high road behind. Captain Paunch, Ned, and several freeholders discovered.

Ned.   Well, gentlemen, I suppose we are all going to the barbecue together.

Capt. Paunch. Indeed, sir, I can assure you, I have no such intention.

Ned.   Not go to your friend Wou'dbe's treat! He's such a pretty fellow, and you like him so well, I wonder you won't go to drink his liquor.

Capt. Paunch. Aye, aye, very strange: but your friends Strutabout and Smallhopes, I like so little as never to take a glass from them, because I shall never pay the price which is always expected for it, by voting against my conscience: I therefore don't go, to avoid being asked for what I won't give.

Ned.   A very disteress motive, truly, but for the matter of that, you've not so much to boast of your friend Wou'dbe, if what I have been told of him is true; for I have heard say, he and the fine beast of a gentleman, Sir John Toddy, have joined interess. Mr. Wou'dbe, I was creditly 'formed, was known for to say, he wouldn't serve for a burgess, unless Sir John was elected with him.

1st Freeholder. What's that you say, neighbor? Has Mr. Wou'dbe and Sir John joined interest?

Ned. Yes, they have; and an't there a clever fellow for ye? A rare burgess you will have, when a fellow gets in, who will go drunk, and be a sleeping in the house! I wish people wouldn't pretend for to hold up their heads so high, who have such friends and associates. There's poor Mr. Smallhopes, who isn't as much attended to, is a very proper gentleman, and is no drunkard, and has no drunken companions.

1st Freeholder. I don't believe it. Mr. Woudbe's a cleverer man than that, and people ought to be ashamed to vent such slanders.

2d Freeholder. So I say: and as we are of one mind, let's go strait, and let Mr. Wou'dbe know it.   [*Exeunt two Freeholders.*

3d Freeholder. If Mr. Wou'dbe did say it, I won't vote for him, that's sartain.

4th Freeholder. Are you sure of it, neighbour? (*To Ned.*)

Ned. Yes, I am sure of it: d'ye think I'd speak such a thing without having good authority?

4th Freeholder. I'm sorry for't; come neighbour, (*to the 3d Freeholder*) this is the worst news that I've heard for a long time.

                    [*Exeunt 3rd. and 4th Freeholder.*

5th Freeholder. I'm glad to hear it. Sir John Toddy is a clever openhearted gentleman as I ever knew, one that won't turn his back upon a poor man, but will take a chearful cup with one as well as another, and it does honour to Mr. Wou'dbe to prefer such a one, to any of your whisslers who han't the heart to be generous, and yet despise poor folks. Huzza! for Mr. Wou'dbe and for Sir John Toddy.

6th Freeholder. I think so too, neighbour. Mr. Wou'dbe, I always thought, was a man of sense, and had larning, as they call it, but he did not love diversion enough, I like him the better for't. Huzza for Mr. Wou'dbe and Sir John Toddy.

Both. Huzza for Mr. Wou'dbe and Sir John Toddy. Wou'dbe and Toddy, for ever, boys!   [*Exeunt.*

Capt. Paunch. The man that heard it is mistaken, for Mr. Wou'dbe never said it.

Ned. I'll lay you a bowl he did.

Capt. Paunch. Done.

Ned. Done, sir, Oh! Jack Sly, Jack Sly.

Jack. (*without*) Halloa.

Enter Jack, saying, "who call'd me? what's your business?"

Ned.   (*winking to Jack*). I have laid a bowl with the Captain here, that
         Mr. Wou'dbe did say, that he would not serve as a buryess un-
         less Sir John Toddy was elected with him.

Jack.   I have heard as much, and more that's little to his credit. He has
         hurt us more than he'll do us good for one while. It's his do-
         ings our levies are so high.

Capt. Paunch. Out upon you, if that's your proof, fetch the bowl. Why
         gentlemen, if I had a mind, I could say as much and more of
         the other candidates. But, gentlemen, 'tis not fair play: don't
         abuse our friend, and we'll let your's alone. Mr. Wou'dbe is a
         clever gentleman, and perhaps so are the rest: let every man
         vote as he pleases, and let's raise no stories to tne prejudice of
         either.

Ned.   Damn me, if I don't speak my mind. Wou'dbe shan't go if I can
         help it, by God, for I boldly say, Mr. Wou'dbe has done us
         more harm than he will ever do us good, (*raising his voice
         very high*).   [*Exeunt into the house,*

Jack.   So say I.   [*Exit after him.*

Capt. Paunch. Go along: bawl your hearts out: nobody will mind you, I
         hope. Well, rejoice that Mr. Wou'dbe is determined still to
         serve us. If he does us no good, he will do us no harm. Mr.
         Strutabout would do very well if he was not such a coxcomb.
         As for Smallhopes, I'd as soon send to New-Market, for a bur-
         gess, as send him, and old Sir John loves tipple too well: egad,
         I'll give Wou'dbe my vote, and throw away the other.

                                                                [*Exit.*

SCENE III.

Wou'dbe's house.

Enter Wou'dbe, looking at a letter.

Wou'dbe. This note gives me information, that the people are much displeased with me for declaring in favour of Sir John Toddy. Who could propagate this report, I know not, but was not this abroad, something else would be reported, as prejudicial to my interest; I must take an opportunity of justifying myself in public.

Enter Ralpho.

Ralpho. Mr. Strutabout waits upon your honour.
Wou'dbe. Desire him to walk in.

Enter Mr. Strutabout.

Strutabout. Mr. Wou'dbe, your servant. Considering the business now in hand, I think you confine yourself too much at home. There are several little reports circulating to your disadvantage, and as a friend, I would advise you to shew yourself to the people, and endeavour to confute them.
Wou'dbe. I believe, sir, I am indebted to my brother candidates, for most of the reports that are propagated to my disadvantage, but I hope, Mr. Strutabout is a man of too much honour, to say anything in my absence, that he cannot make appear.
Strutabout. That you may depend on, sir. But there are some who are so intent upon taking your place, that they will stick at nothing to obtain their ends.
Wou'dbe. Are you in the secret, sir?
Strutabout. So far, sir, that I have had overtures from Mr. Smallhopes and his friends, to join my interest with their's, against you. This, I rejected with disdain, being conscious that you were the properest person to serve the county; but when Smallhopes told me he intended to prejudice your interest by scatering a few stories among the people to your disadvantage, it raised my blood to such a pitch, that had he not promised me to be silent, I believe I should have chastised him for you myself.

Wou'dbe. If, sir, you were so far my friend, I am obliged to you: though whatever report he is the author of, will, I am certain, gain little credit with the people.

Strutabout. I believe so; and therefore, if you are willing, we'll join our interests together, and soon convince the fellow, that by attacking you he has injured himself.

Wou'dbe. So far from joining with you, or any body else, or endeavouring to procure a vote for you, I am determined never to ask a vote for myself, or receive one that is unduly obtained.

Enter Ralpho.

Ralpho. Master, rare news, here's our neighbour Guzzle, as drunk as ever Chief Justice Cornelius[2] was upon the bench.

Wou'dbe. That's no news, Ralpho: but do you call it rare news that a creature in the shape of man, and endued with the faculties of reason, should so far debase the workmanship of heaven by making his carcase a receptacle for such pollution?

Ralpho. Master, you are hard upon neighbour Guzzle: our justices gets drunk, and why not poor Guzzle? But sir, he wants to see you.

Wou'dbe. Tell him to come in. (*exit Ralpho*). All must be made wetcome now.

Re-enter Ralpho and Guzzle, with an empty bottle.

Guzzle. Ha! Mr. Wou'dbe, how is it?

Wou'dbe. I'm something more in my senses than you, John, tho' not so sensible as you would have me, I suppose.

Guzzle. If I can make you sensible how much I want my bottle filled, and how much I shall love the contents, it's all the senses I desire you to have.

Ralpho. If I may be allowed to speak, neighbour Guzzle, you are wrong; his honour sits up for a burgess, and should have five senses at least.

Guzzle. Five senses! how, what five?

Ralpho. Why, neighbour, you know, eating, drinking, and sleeping are three; t'other two are best known to myself.

Wou'dbe. I'm sorry Mr. Guzzle, you are so ignorant of the necessary qualifications of a member of the house of burgesses.

Guzzle. Why, you old dog, I knew before Ralpho told me. To convince you, eating, drinking, and sleeping, are three; fighting and lying are t'others.

<hr>

2 When Munford first held a post on the county commission, Cornelius Carghill was senior magistrate of Lunenburg County; in 1761 he was removed for cursing and drinking.

Wou'dbe. Why fighting and lying?

Guzzle. Why, because you are not fit for a burgess, unless you'll fight;
    suppose a man that values himself upon boxing, should stand
    in the lobby, ready cock'd and prim'd, and knock you down,
    and bung up both your eyes for a fortnight, you'd be ashamed
    to shew your face in the house, and be living at our expence
    all the time.

Wou'dbe. Why lying?

Guzzle. Because, when you have been at Williamsburg, for six or seven
    weeks, under pretence of serving your county, and come back,
    says I to you, what news? None at all, says you; what have
    you been about? says I,—says you—and so you must tell
    some damned lie sooner than say you have been doing nothing.

Wou'dbe. No, Guzzle, I'll make it a point of duty to dispatch the busi-
    ness, and my study to promote the good of my county.

Guzzle. Yes, damn it, you all promise mighty fair, but the devil a bit do
    you perform; there's Strutabout, now, he'll promise to move
    mountains. He'll make the rivers navigable, and bring the tide
    over the tops of the hills for a vote.

Strutabout. You may depend, Mr. Guzzle, I'll perform whatever I prom-
    ise.

Guzzle. I don't believe it, damn me if I like you. (*looking angry.*)

Wou'dbe. Don't be angry, John, let our actions hereafter be the test of
    our inclinations to serve you.   [*Exit Struabout.*

Guzzle. Agreed, Mr. Wou'dbe, but that fellow that slunk off just now,
    I've no opinion of.

Wou'dbe. (*Looking about*) what, is Mr. Strutabout gone? why, surely,
    Guzzle, you did not put him to flight?

Guzzle. I suppose I did, but no matter, (*holding up his bottle, and look-
    ing at it,*) my bottle never was so long a filling in this house
    before; surely there's a leak in the bottom, (*looks at it again*).

Wou'dbe. What have you got in your bottle, John, a lizard?

Guzzle. Yes, a very uncommon one, and I want a little rum put to it, to
    preserve it.

Wou'dbe. Hav'n't you one in your belly, John?

Guzzle. A dozen, I believe, by their twisting when I mentioned the rum.

Wou'dbe. Would you have rum to preserve them, too?

Guzzle. Yes, yes, Mr. Wou'dbe, by all means; but, why so much talk
    about it; if you intend to do it, do it at once, man, for I am in a
    damnable hurry.

Wou'dbe. Do what? Who are to be burgesses, John?

Guzzle. Who are to be what? (*looking angry*).

Wou'd be. Burgesses, who are you for?

Guzzle. For the first man that fills my bottle: so Mr Wou'dbe, your ser-
    vant.   [*Exit Guzzle.*

Wou'dbe. Ralpho, go after him, and fill his bottle.

Ralpho. Master, we ought to be careful of the rum, else 'twill not hold
    out, (aside) it's always a feast or a famine with us; master has
    just got a little Jamaica for his own use, and now he must spill
    it, and spare it till there's not a drop left.   *[Exit*

Wou'dbe. (*pulling out his watch.*) 'Tis now the time a friend of mine
    has appointed for me to meet the freeholders at a barbecue;
    well, I find, in order to secure a seat in our august senate, 'tis
    necessary a man should either be a slave or a fool; a slave to
    the people, for the privilege of serving them, and a fool him-
    self, for thus begging a troublesome and expensive employ-
    ment.

> To sigh, while toddy-toping sots rejoice,
> To see you paying for their empty voice,
> From morn to night your humble head decline,
> To gain an honour that is justly thine,
> Intreat a fool, who's your's at this day's treat,
> And next another's, if another's meat,
> Is all the bliss a candidate acquires,
> In all his wishes, or his vain desires.

                                                          [Exit.

END OF THE FIRST ACT.

ACT II.   SCENE I.

*A race-field, a bullock, and several hogs barbecued. Twist, Stern,
Prize, Lucy, Catharine, and Sarah, sitting on four fence rails.*

Twist.   Well, gentlemen, what do you think of Mr. Strutabout and Mr.
          Smallhopes? It seems one of the old ones declines, and
          t'other, I believe might as well, if what neighbour Sly says is
          true.

Stern.   Pray, gentlemen, what plausible objection have you against Mr.
          Wou'dbe? He's a clever civil gentleman as any, and as far as
          my poor weak capacity can go, he's a man of as good learn-
          ing, and knows the punctilios of behaving himself with the
          best of them.

Prize.   Wou'dbe, for sartin, is a civil gentleman, but he can't speak his
          mind so boldly as Mr. Strutabout, and commend me to a man
          that will speak his mind freely;—I say.

Lucy.   Well, commend me to Mr. Wou'dbe, I say,—I nately like the
          man; he's mighty good to all his poor neighbours, and when
          he comes into a poor body's house, he's so free and so funny,
          isn't he, old man? (*speaking to Twist*).

Twist.   A little too free sometimes, faith; he was funny when he wanted
          to see the colour of your garters; wa'nt he?

Lucy.   Oh! for shame, husband. Mr. Wou'dbe has no more harm about
          him than a sucking babe; at least, if he has, I never saw it.

Twist.   Nor felt it, I hope; but wife, you and I, you know, could never
          agree about burgesses.

Lucy.   If the wives were to vote, I believe they would make a better
          choice than their husbands.

Twist.   You'd be for the funnyest—wou'dn't you?

Lucy.   Yes, faith; and the wittiest, and prettiest, and the wisest, and the
          best too; you are all for ugly except when you chose me.

Catharine. Well done, Lucy, you are right, girl. If we were all to speak
          to our old men as freely as you do, there would be better do-
          ings.

Stern.   Perhaps not, Kate.

Catharine. I am sure there would; for if a clever gentleman, now-a-
          days, only gives a body a gingercake in a civil way, you are
          sullen for a week about it. Remember when Mr. Wou'dbe
          promised Molly a riband and a pair of buckles, you would not
          let the poor girl have 'em: but you take toddy from him;—yes,
          and you'll drink a little too much, you know, Richard.

Stern. Well, it's none of our costs, if I do.

Catharine. Husband, you know Mr. Wou'dbe is a clever gentleman; he has been a good friend to us.

Stern. I agree to it, and can vote for him without your dash.

Sarah. I'll be bound when it comes to the pinch, they'll all vote for him: won't you old man? He stood for our George, when our neighbor refused us.

Prize. Mr. Wou'dbe's a man well enough in his neighbourhood, and he may have learning, as they say he has, but he don't shew it like Mr. Strutabout.

Enter Guzzle, and several freeholders.

Guzzle. Your servant, gentlemen; (*shakes hands all round*) we have got fine weather, thank God: how are crops with you? We are very dry in our parts.

Twist. We are very dry here; Mr. Guzzle, where's your friend Sir John, and Mr. Wou'dbe? They are to treat to-day, I hear.

Guzzle. I wish I could see it, but there are more treats besides their's; where's your friend Mr. Strutabout? I heard we were to have a treat from Smallhopes and him to-day.

Twist. Fine times, boys. Some of them had better keep their money; I'll vote for no man but to my liking.

Guzzle. If I may be so bold, pray, which way is your liking?

Twist. Not as your's is, I believe; but nobody shall know my mind till the day.

Guzzle. Very good, Mr. Twist; nobody, I hope, will put themselves to the trouble to ask.

Twist. You have taken the trouble already.

Guzzle. No harm, I hope, sir.

Twist. None at all, sir: Yonder comes Sir John, and quite sober, as I live.

Enter Sir John Toddy.

Sir John. Gentlemen and ladies, your servant, hah! My old friend Prize, how goes it? How does your wife and children do?

Sarah. At your service, sir. (*making a low courtsey.*)

Prize. (*aside*) How the devil come he to know me so well, and never spoke to me before in his life?

Guzzle. (*whispering Sir John*) Dick Stern.

Sir John. Hah! Mr. Stern, I'm proud to see you; I hope your family are well; how many children? Does the good woman keep to the old stroke?

Catharine. Yes, an't please your honour, I hope my lady's well with your honour.

Sir John. At your service, madam.

Guzzle. (*whispering Sir John*) Roger Twist.

Sir John. Hah! Mr. Roger Twist! Your servant, sir. I hope your wife and children are well.

Twist. There's my wife. I have no children, at your service.

Sir John. A pretty girl: why, Roger, if you don't do better, you must call an old fellow to your assistance.

Twist. I have enough to assist me, without applying to you, sir.

Sir John. No offence, I hope, sir; excuse my freedom.

Twist. None at all, sir; Mr. Wou'dbe is ready to befriend me in that way at any time.

Sir John. Not in earnest, I hope, sir; tho' he's a damn'd fellow, I believe.

Lucy. Why, Roger, if you talk at this rate, people will think you are jealous; for shame of yourself.

Twist. For shame of yourself, you mean.

Guzzle. A truce, a truce—here comes Mr. Wou'dbe.

Enter Mr. Wou'dbe.

Wou'dbe. Gentlemen, your servant. Why, Sir John, you have entered the list, it seems; and are determined to whip over the ground, if you are treated with a distance.

Sir John. I'm not to be distanc'd by you, or a dozen such.

Wou'dbe. There's nothing like courage upon these occasions; but you were out when you chose me to ride for you, Sir John.

Sir John. Let's have no more of your algebra, nor proverbs, here.

Guzzle. Come, gentlemen, you are both friends, I hope.

Wou'dbe. While Sir John confined himself to his bottle and dogs, and moved only in his little circle of pot-companions, I could be with him; but since his folly has induced him to offer himself a candidate for a place, for which he is not fit, I must say, I despise him. The people are of opinion, that I favour this undertaking of his; but I now declare, he is not the man I wish the people to elect.

Guzzle. Pray, sir, who gave you a right to choose for us?

Wou'dbe. I have no right to choose for you; but I have a right to give my opinion: especially when I am the supposed author of Sir John's folly.

Guzzle. Perhaps he's no greater fool than some others.

Wou'dbe. It would be ungrateful in you, Mr. Guzzle, not to speak in favour of Sir John; for you have stored away many gallons of his liquor in that belly of your's.

Guzzle. And he's the cleverer gentleman for it; is not he, neighbours?

1st Freeholder. For sartin; it's no disparagement to drink with a poor fellow.

2d Freeholder. No more it is, tho' some of the quality are mighty proud that way.

3d Freeholder. Mr. Wou'dbe shou'd'n't speak so freely against that.

Twist. Mr. Wou'dbe.

Wou'dbe. Sir.

Twist. We have heard a sartin report, that you and Sir John have joined interest.

Wou'dbe. Well; do you believe it?

Twist. Why, it don't look much like it now, Mr. Wou'dbe; but, mayhap, it's only a copy of your countenance.

Wou'dbe. You may put what construction you please upon my behaviour, gentlemen; but I assure you, it never was my intention to join with Sir John, or any one else.

Twist. Moreover, I've heard a reasonable man say he could prove you were the cause of these new taxes.

Wou'dbe. Do you believe that too? Or can you believe that it's in the power of any individual member to make a law himself? If a law is enacted that is displeasing to the people, it has the concurrence of the whole legislative body, and my vote for, or against it, is of little consequence.

Guzzle. And what the devil good do you do then?

Wou'dbe. As much as I have abilities to do.

Guzzle. Suppose, Mr. Wou'dbe, we were to want you to get the price of rum lower'd—wou'd you do it?

Wou'dbe. I cou'd not.

Guzzle. Huzza for Sir John! He has promised to do it, huzza for Sir John!

Twist. Suppose, Mr. Wou'dbe, we should want this tax taken off— cou'd you do it?

Wou'dbe. I could not.

Twist. Huzza for Mr. Strutabout! he's damn'd, if he don't. Huzza for Mr. Strutabout!

Stern. Suppose, Mr. Wou'dbe, we that live over the river should want to come to church on this side; is it not very hard we should pay ferryage when we pay as much to the church as you do?

Wou'dbe. Very hard.

Stern. Suppose we were to petition the assembly could you get us clear of that expence?

Wou'dbe. I believe it to be just; and make no doubt but it would pass into a law.

Stern. Will you do it?

Wou'dbe. I will endeavour to do it.

Stern. Huzza for Mr. Wou'dbe! Wou'dbe forever!

Prize.   Why don't you burgesses, do something with the damn'd pick-
            ers? If we have a hogshead of tobacco refused, away it goes to
            them; and after they have twisted up the best of it for their
            own use, and taken as much as will pay them for their trouble,
            the roof planter has little for his share.
Wou'dbe. There are great complaints against them; and I believe the as-
            sembly will take them under consideration.
Prize.   Will you vote against ehem?
Wou'dbe. I will, if they deserve it.
Prize.   Huzza for Mr. Wou'dbe! You shall go, old fellow; don't be
            afraid; I'll warrant it.
                        [*Exeunt severally; some huzzaing for Mr. Wou'dbe*
                                        —some for Sir John
                                        —some for Mr. Strutabout.

SCENE II.

Another part of the field.

*Mr. Strutabout, Mr. Smallhopes, and a number of freeholders round
them.*

1st Freeholder. Huzza for Mr. Strutabout!
2d Freeholder. Huzza for Mr. Smallhopes!
3d Freeholder. Huzza for Mr. Smallhopes and Mr. Strutabout!
4th Freeholder. Huzza for Mr. Strutabout and Mr. Smallhopes!
                                        [*Exeunt, huzzaing.*

Enter Guzzle, drunk.

Guzzle.   Huzza for Sir John Toddy, the cleverest gentleman—the finest
            gentleman that ever was (*hickuping.*)

Enter Mrs. Guzzle, drunk.

Mrs. Guzzle. Where's my drunken beast of a husband? (*hickups*) Oh
            John Guzzle, Oh John Guzzle.
Guzzle.   What the devil do you want?
Mrs. Guzzle. Why don't you go home you drunken beast? Lord bless
            me, how the gingerbread has given me the hickup.
Guzzle.   Why, Joan, you have made too—free with the bottle—I believe.
Mrs. Guzzle. I make free with the bottle—you drunken sot!—Well,
            well, the gingerbread has made me quite giddy.

Guzzle. Hold up, Joan, don't fall—(*Mrs. Guzzle falls.*) The devil, you will? Joan! Why woman, what's the matter? Are you drunk?

Mrs. Guzzle. Drunk! you beast! No, quite sober; but very sick with eating gingerbread.

Guzzle. For shame, Joan get up—(*offers to help her up, and falls upon her.*)

Mrs. Guzzle. Oh Lord! John! You've almost killed me.

Guzzle. Not I—I'll get clear of you as fast as I can.

Mrs. Guzzle. Oh John, I shall die, I shall die.

Guzzle. Very well, you'll die a pleasant death, then.

Mrs. Guzzle. Oh Lord! How sick! How sick!

Guzzle. Oh Joan Guzzle! Oh Joan Guzzle!—Why don't you go home, you drunken beast. Lord bless me, how the gingerbread has given me the hickup.

Mrs. Guzzle. Pray, my dear John, help me up.

Guzzle. Pray, my dear Joan, get sober first.

Mrs. Guzzle. Pray John, help me up.

Guzzle. Pray, Joan, go to sleep; and when I am as drunk as you, I'll come and take your place. Farewell, Joan. Huzza for Sir John Toddy! [*Exit huzzaing.*

Scene changes to another part of the field. Strutabout, Smallhopes, and freeholders.

Strutabout. Gentlemen—I'm much obliged to you for your good intentions; I make no doubt but (with the assistance of my friend Mr. Smallhopes) I shall be able to do every thing you have requested. Your grievances shall be redress'd; and all your petitions heard.

Freeholders. Huzza for Mr. Strutabout and Mr. Smallhopes!

Enter Mr. Wou'dbe.

Wou'dbe. Gentlemen, your servant; you seem happy in a circle of your friends; I hope my company is not disagreeable.

Strutabout. It can't be very agreeable to those you have treated so ill.

Smallhopes. You have used me ill, and all this company, by God—

Wou'dbe. If I have, Gentlemen, I am sorry for it; but it never was my intention to treat any person ungenteely.

Smllhopes. You be damn'd; you're a turn-coat, by God.

Wou'dbe. Your abuse will never have any weight with me: neither do I regard your oaths or imprecations. In order to support a weak cause, you swear to what requires better proof than your assertions.

Smallhopes. Where's your friend, Sir John Toddy? He's a pretty fel-
      low, an't he, and be damn'd to you; you recommend him to
      the people, don't you?

Wou'dbe. No, sir; I should be as blamable to recommend Sir John, as
      you, and your friend there (pointing to Strutabout) in recom-
      mending one another.

Strutabout. Sir, I am as capable of serving the people as yourself; and
      let me tell you, sir, my sole intention in offering myself is that
      I may redress the many and heavy grievances you have im-
      posed upon this poor county.

Wou'dbe. Poor, indeed, when you are believed, or when coxcombs and
      jockies can impose themselves upon it for men of learning.

1st Freeholder. Well, its no use; Mr. Wou'dbe is too hard for them
      both.

2d Freeholder. I think so too: why Strutabout! Speak up, old fellow, or
      you'll lose ground.

Strutabout. I'll lay you fifty pounds I'm elected before you.

Wou'dbe. Betting will not determine it; and therefore I shall not lay.

Strutabout. I can lick you, Wou'dbe. (*beginning to strip.*)

Wou'dbe. You need not strip to do it; for you intend to do it with your
      tongue, I suppose.

Smallhopes. (*clapping Strutabout upon the back*) Well done Stru-
      tabout,—you can do it, by God. Don't be afraid, you shan't be
      hurt; damn me if you shall, (*strips.*)

Wou'dbe. What! Gentlemen, do they who aspire to the first posts in our
      county, and who have ambition to become legislators and to
      take upon themselves part of the guidance of the state, submit
      their naked bodies to public view, as if they were malefactors
      or, for some crimes, condemned to the whipping-post?

Smallhopes. Come on, damn ye; and don't preach your damn'd prov-
      erbs here.

Wou'dbe. Are the candidates to fight for their seats in the house of bur-
      gesses? If so, perhaps I may stand as good a chance to suc-
      ceed, as you.

Smallhopes. I can lick you, by God. Come on, if you dare—(*capering
      about.*)

1st Freeholder. Up to him—I'll stand by you. (*to Wou'dbe.*)

2d Freeholder. They are not worth your notice, Mr. Wou'dbe; but if
      you have a mind to try yourself, I'll see fair play.

Wou'dbe. When I think they have sufficiently exposed themselves, I'll
      explain the opinion I have of them, with the end of my cane.

Smallhopes. Up to him, damn ye, (*pushing Strutabout.*)

Strutabout. You need not push me, I can fight without being pushed to
      it; fight yourself, if you are so fond of it. (*putting on his
      cloaths.*)

Smallhopes. Nay, if you are for that, and determined to be a coward, Mr. Strutabout, I can't help it; but damn me if I ever hack. (*putting on his cloaths.*)

Wou'dbe. So you are both scared, gentlemen, without a blow, or an angry look! ha, ha, ha! Well, gentlemen, you have escaped a good caning, and though you are not fit for burgesses, you'll make good soldiers; for you are excellent at a retreat.

1st Freeholder. Huzza for Mr. Wou'dbe!

2d Freeholder. Huzza for Mr. Wou'dbe!

Enter Guzzle.

Guzzle. Huzza for Sir John Toddy! Toddy (*hickups*) forever, boys!

Enter Sir John, drunk.

Guzzle. Here he comes—as fine gentleman, tho' I say it, as the best of them.

Sir John. So I am, John, as clever a fellow (hickups) as the famous Mr. Wou'dbe, tho' I (*hickups*) say it.

Strutabout. There's a pretty fellow to be a burgess, gentlemen: lord, what a drunken beast it is.

Sir John. What beast, pray? Am I a beast?

Strutabout. Yes, Sir John, you are a beast, and you may take the name of what beast you please; so your servant, my dear.

[*Exeunt Strutabout and Smallhopes.*

Wou'dbe. Except an ass, Sir John, for that he's entitled to.

Sir John. Thank you, sir.

Wou'dbe. A friend in need, Sir John, as the proverb says, is a friend indeed.

Sir John. I thank you; I know you are my friend (hickups) Mr. Wou'dbe, if you'd speak your mind—I know you are.

Wou'dbe. How do you know it, Sir John?

Sir John. Did not you take my part just now, Mr. Wou'dbe? (*hickups*) I know it.

Wou'dbe. I shall always take your part, Sir John, when you are imposed upon by a greater scoundrel than yourself, and when you pretend to what you are not fit for, I shall always oppose you.

Sir John. Well, Mr. Wou'dbe, an't I as fitten a (*hickups*) man as either of those?

Wou'dbe. More so, Sir John, for they are knaves; and you, Sir John, are an honest blockhead.

Sir John. Is that in my favour, or not, John? (*to Guzzle.*)

Guzzle.   In your favour, by all means; for (*hickups*) he says you are honest. Huzza for Mr. Wou'dbe and the honest (*hickups*) Sir John Blockhead.

Enter Ralpho—gives a letter to Wou'dbe.

Wou'dbe. (*Reads*)—this is good news indeed.
1st Freeholder. Huzza for Mr. Wou'dbe!
2d Freeholder. Huzza for Mr. Wou'dbe!
Guzzle. Huzza for the honest Sir John Block—(*hickups*) head.
Wou'dbe. Silence, gentlemen, and I'll read a letter to you, that (I don't doubt) will give you great pleasure. (*he reads*) Sir, I have been informed that the scoundrels who opposed us last election (not content with my resignation) are endeavouring to undermine you in the good opinion of the people: It has warmed my blood, and again call'd my thoughts from retirement; speak this to the people, and let them know I intend to stand a poll, &c. Your's affectionately.   WORTHY.
Freeholders. Huzza for Mr. Wou'dbe and Mr. Worthy!
Sir John. Huzza for Mr. Worthy and Mr. Wou'dbe! (hickups) I'm not so fitten as they, and therefore gentlemen I recline. (hickups) Yes, gentlemen (*staggering about*) I will; for I am not (hickups) so fitten as they. (*falls*).
Guzzle. Huzza for the drunken Sir John Toddy. (*hickups*).
Sir John. Help me up John—do, John, help.
Guzzle. No, Sir John, stay, and I'll fetch my wife, Joan, and lay—her along side of you.   [*Exit.*
Wou'dbe. Ralpho.
Ralpho. Sir.
Wou'dbe. Take care of Sir John, least any accident should befall him.
Ralpho. Yes, sir.
   [*Exeunt Wou'dbe and freeholders, huzzaing for Wou'dbe and Worthy.*

Enter Guzzle, with his wife in his arms.

Guzzle.   Here, Sir John, here's my wife fast asleep, to keep you company, and as drunk as a sow. (*throws her upon Sir John, and returns to one side.*)
Sir John. Oh Lord! You've broke my bones.
Joan.   (*waking*) John! John! (*punching Sir John*) Get up; (*looking round, sees Sir John*) what have we here? Lord, what would our John give to know this? He would have reason to be jealous of me, then!

Enter Guzzle.

Guzzle. Well, Joan, are you sober?
Joan. (*getting up*) How came that man to be lying with me? It's some of your doings, I'm sure; that you may have an excuse to be jealous of me.
Guzzle. I want no excuse for that, child.
Joan. What brought him there?
Guzzle. The same that brought you, child; rum, sugar, and water.
Joan. Well, well, as I live, I thought it was you, and that we were in our own clean sweet bed. Lord! how I tremble for fear he should have done what you do, sometimes, John.
Guzzle. I never do any thing when I am drunk. Sir John and you have done more than that, I believe.
Joan. Don't be jealous, John; it will ruin us both.
Guzzle. I am very jealous of that.
Joan. If you are, I'll beat the cruel beast that is the cause of it 'till he satisfies you I am innocent.
Guzzle. Don't, Joan, it will make me more jealous.
Joan. I will, I tell you I will. (*beats Sir John, who all the time cries murder, help, help!*)
Ralpho. Stop, madam, this gentleman is in my care; and you must not abuse him.
Mrs. Guzzle. I will, and you too, you rascal. (*beats him first, and then Sir John.*)
Ralpho. Peace, stop, madam, peace, peace.
Sir John. Oh lord! Help, John, for God's sake, help.
Ralpho. Do as you please, madam; do as you please. (*runs off*).
Joan. (*beating Sir John*) I'll learn you to cuckold a man without letting his wife know it.
Sir John. Help, murder! help.
Guzzle. (*taking hold of Joan*) Stop, Joan, I'm satisfied—quite satisfied.
Joan. What fellow is it?
Guzzle. Sir John Toddy, our good friend; Oh, Joan, you should not have beat poor Sir John; he is as drunk as you and I were, Joan. Oh! poor Sir John. (*cries.*)
Joan. Good lack, why did'nt you tell me? I would have struck you as soon as him, John. Don't be angry, good Sir John; I did not know you.
Sir John. It's well enough: help me out of the mire, neighbours, and I'll forget and forgive.
Guzzle. Yes, Sir John, and so we will. (*they help him up.*) Come, Sir John, let's go home; this is no place for us: come Joan.
                    [*Exeunt Guzzle and Joan, supporting Sir John.*

SCENE III.

Another part of the field.

Enter Wou'dbe and Ralpho.

Wou'dbe. Where's Sir John?

Ralpho. In the hands of a woman, sir; and as I left him in such good hands, I thought there was no farther occasion for my attendance.

Wou'dbe. Are you sure he'll be taken care of?

Ralpho. Yes, the lady, an't please your honour, seemed devilish kind to him.

Wou'dbe. See that you have all ready; its high time we thought of going home, if we intend there to-night.

Ralpho. All shall be ready, sir.   [*Exit Ralpho.*

Wou'dbe. Well, I've felt the pulse of all the leading men, and find they beat still for Worthy and myself. Strutabout and Smallhopes fawn and cringe in so abject a manner for the few votes they get that I'm in hopes they'll be soon heartily despised.

> The prudent candidate who hopes to rise,
> Ne'er deigns to hide it, in a mean disguise.
> Will, to his place, with moderation slide,
> And win his way, or not resist the tide.
> The fool, aspiring to bright honour's post,
> In noise, in shouts, and tumults oft, is lost.

[*Exit.*

END OF THE SECOND ACT.

ACT III. SCENE I.

Wou'dbe's house.

Enter Wou'dbe and Worthy.

Wou'dbe. Nothing could have afforded me more pleasure than your letter; I read it to the people and can with pleasure assure you it gave them infinite satisfaction.

Worthy. My sole motive in declaring myself was to serve you, and if I am the means of your gaining your election with honour, I shall be satisfied.

Wou'dbe. You have always been extremely kind, sir, but I could not enjoy the success I promised myself without your participation.

Worthy. I have little inclination to the service; you know my aversion to public life, Wou'dbe, and how little I have ever courted the people for the troublesome office they have hitherto imposed upon me.

Wou'dbe. I believe you enjoy as much domestic happiness as any person and that your aversion to a public life proceeds from the pleasure you find at home. But, sir, it surely is the duty of every man who has abilities to serve his country, to take up the burden, and bear it with patience.

Worthy. I know it is needless to argue with you upon this head: you are determined I shall serve with you, I find.

Wou'dbe. I am; and therefore let's take the properest methods to insure success.

Worthy. What would you propose?

Wou'dbe. Nothing more than for you to shew yourself to the people.

Worthy. I'll attend you where ever you please.

Wou'dbe. To-morrow being the day of election, I have invited most of the principal freeholders to breakfast with me in their way to the courthouse. I hope you'll favour us with your company.

Worthy. I will; till then, adieu.   [*Exit Worthy.*

Wou'dbe. I shall expect you. It would give me great pleasure if Worthy would be more anxious than he appears to be upon this occasion; conscious of his abilities and worth, he scorns to ask a vote for any person but me; well, I must turn the tables on him, and solicit as strongly in his favour.

'Tis said self-interest is the secret aim,
Of those uniting under Friendship's name.

How true this maxim is, let others prove—
Myself I'd punish for the man I love.

[Exit Wou'dbe.

SCENE II.

Mr. Julip's House

Enter Captain Paunch and Mr. Julip.

Capt. Paunch. Well, neighbour, I have come to see you on purpose to
know how votes went at the treat yesterday.
Julip.   I was not there; but I've seen neighbour Guzzle this morning, and
he says, Sir John gives the matter up to Mr. Worthy and Mr.
Wou'dbe.
Capt. Paunch. Mr. Worthy! Does he declare? Huzza, my boys! Well,
I'm proud our county may choose two without being obliged
to have one of those jackanapes at the head of it, faith: Who
are you for now, neighbour?
Julip.   I believe I shall vote for the two old ones, and tho' I said I was
for Sir John, it was because I lik'd neither of the others; but
since Mr. Worthy will serve us, why, to be sartin its our duty
to send Wou'dbe and him.
Capt. Paunch. Hah, faith, now you speak like a man; you are a man after my own heart: give me your hand.
Julip.   Here it is; Wou'dbe and Worthy, I say.
Capt. Paunch. Done, but who comes yonder? Surely, it's not Mr. Worthy! 'Tis, I declare.

Enter Mr. Worthy.

Worthy. Gentlemen, your servant, I hope your families are well.
Capt. Paunch. At your service, sir.
Worthy. I need not, I suppose, gentlemen, inform you that I have entered the list with my old competitors and have determined to
stand a poll at the next election. If you were in the croud yesterday, my friend Wou'dbe, I doubt not, made a declaration of
my intentions to the people.
Capt. Paunch. We know it, thank heaven, Mr. Worthy, tho' neither of
us were there: as I did not like some of the candidates, I did
not choose to be persecuted for a vote that I was resolved
never to bestow upon them.

Julip.   My rule is never to taste of a man's liquor unless I'm his friend, and therefore, I stay'd at home.

Worthy. Well, my honest friend, I am proud to find that you still preserve your usual independence. Is it possible Captain, that the people can be so misled, as to reject Wou'dbe, and elect Strutabout in his room?

Capt. Paunch. You know, Mr. Worthy, how it is: as long as the liquor is running, so long they'll be Mr. Strutabout's friends, but when the day comes, I'm thinking it will be another case.

Worthy. I'm sorry, my countymen, for the sake of a little toddy, can be induced to behave in a manner so contradictory to the candour and integrity which always should prevail among mankind.

Capt. Paunch. It's so, sir, you may depend upon it.

Julip.   I'm a thinking it is.

Worthy. Well, gentlemen, will you give me leave to ask you: how far you think my declaring will be of service to Mr. Wou'dbe?

Capt. Paunch. Your declaring has already silenced Sir John Toddy; and I doubt not, but Strutabout and Smallhopes will lose many votes by it.

Worthy. Has Sir John declined? Poor Sir John is a weak man, but he has more virtues to recommend him than either of the others.

Julip.   So I think, Mr. Worthy, and I'll be so bold as to tell you that had you not set up, Mr. Wou'dbe and Sir John should have had my vote.

Worthy. Was I a constituent, instead of a candidate, I should do the same.

Julip.   Well, captain, you see I was not so much to blame.

Capt. Paunch. Sir John may be honest, but he is no fitter for that place than myself.

Julip.   Suppose he was not—if he was the best that offered to serve us, should not we choose him?

Worthy. Yes, surely: Well, my friends, I'm now on my way to breakfast at Mr. Wou'dbe's, but I hope to meet you at the courthouse today.

Both.   Aye, aye, depend upon us.   [*Exit Worthy.*

Capt. Paunch. Well, neighbour, I hope things now go on better; I like the present appearance.

Julip.   So do I.

Capt. Paunch. Do all you can, old fellow.

Julip.   I will.

Capt. Paunch. I hope you will, neighbour. I wish you well.

Julip.   You the same.   [*shake hands, and exeunt.*

Scene III.

Woud'be's house, a long breakfast table set out. Wou'dbe, Worthy, Capt. Paunch, Mr. Julip, Twist, Stern, Prize, and other freeholders; several negroes go backwards and forwards, bringing in the breakfast.

1st Freeholder. Give us your hand, neighbour Worthy; I'm extremely glad to see thee with all my heart: So my heart of oak, you are willing to give your time and trouble once more to the service of your country.

Worthy. Your kindness does me honour, and if my labours be productive of good to my country, I shall deem myself fortunate.

2d Freeholder. Still the same sensible man I always thought him. Damn it, now if every county cou'd but send such a burgess, what a noble house we should have?

3d Freeholder. We shall have no polling now, but all will be for the same, I believe. Here's neighbour Twist, who was resolute for Strutabout, I don't doubt, will vote for Mr. Worthy and Mr. Wou'dbe.

Twist. Yes, that I will: what could I do better?

All. Aye, so will we all.

Wou'dbe. Gentlemen, for your forwardness in favour of my good friend Worthy, my sincere thanks are but a poor expression in the pleasure I feel. For my part, your esteem I shall always attribute more to his than my own desert. But come, let us sit down to breakfast. All is ready I believe; and you're heartily welcome to batchelor's quarters. (*they all sit down to the table, he asks each of the company which they prefer, coffee, tea, or chocolate, and each chooses to his liking; he pours out, and the servants carry it around.*)

Worthy. Gentlemen, will any of you have a part of this fine salt shad? (*they answer, yes, if you please; and he helps them.*)

Capt. Paunch. This warm toast and butter is very fine, and the shad gives it an excellent flavour.

Mr. Julip. Boy, give me the spirit. This chocolate, me thinks, wants a little lacing to make it admirable. (*the servants bring it.*)

Prize. Mr. Wou'dbe, do your fishing places succeed well this year?

Wou'dbe. Better than they've been known for some seasons.

Stern. I'm very glad of it: for then I can get my supply from you.

Mr. Julip. Neighbour Stalk, how do crops stand with you?

1st Freeholder. Indifferently well, I thank you; how are you?

Mr. Julip. Oh, very well! We crop it gloriously.

Wou'dbe. You have not breakfasted yet, neighbour; give me leave to help you to another dish.

2d Freeholder. Thank ye, sir, but enough's as good as a feast.

Capt. Paunch. (*looking at his watch.*) I'm afraid we shall be late, they ought to have begun before now.

Wou'dbe. Our horses are at the gate, and we have not far to go.

Freeholders all. Very well, we've all breakfasted. (*they rise from table and the servants take away.*)

1st Freeholder. Come along, my friends, I long to see your triumph. Huzza for Wou'dbe and Worthy!   [*Exit huzzaing.*

SCENE IV.

The Court-house yard.

The door open, and a number of freeholders seen crowding within.

1st Freeholder. (*to a freeholder coming out of the house*) How do votes go, neighbour? For Wou'dbe and Worthy?

2d Freeholder. Aye, aye, they're just come, and sit upon the bench, and yet all the votes are for them. 'Tis quite a hollow thing. The poll will be soon over. The people crowd so much and vote so fast, you can hardly turn around.

1st Freeholder. How do Strutabout and Smallhopes look? Very doleful, I reckon.

2d Freeholder. Like a thief under the gallows.

3d Freeholder. There you must be mistaken, neighbour; for two can't be like one.

1st and 2d Freeholder. Ha, ha, ha,—a good joke, a good joke.

3d Freeholder. Not so good neither, when the subject made it so easy.

1st and 2d Freeholders. Better and better, ha, ha, ha. Huzza for Worthy and Wou'dbe and confusion to Strutabout and Smallhopes!

Enter Guzzle.

Guzzle. Huzza for Wou'dbe and Worthy! And huzza for Sir John Toddy tho' he reclines!

1st Freeholder. So Guzzle, your friend Sir John reclines, does he? I think he does right.

Guzzle. You think he does right! Pray sir, what right have you to think about it? Nobody but a fool would kick a fallen man lower.

1st Freeholder. Sir, I won't be called a fool by any man, I'll have you to know, sir.

Guzzle. Then you ought'nt to be one; but here's at ye, adrat ye, if ye're
    for a quarrel. Sir John Toddy would have stood a good chance,
    and I'll maintain it; come on, damn ye.
1st Freeholder. Oh! As for fighting, there I'm your servant; a drunkard
    is as bad to fight as a madman. (*runs off.*)
Guzzle. Houroa, houroa, you see no body so good at a battle as a
    staunch toper. The milksops are afraid of them to a man.
3d Freeholder. You knew he was a coward before you thought proper
    to attack him; if you think yourself so brave, try your hand
    upon me, and you'll find you're mistaken.
Guzzle. For the matter of that, I'm the best judge myself; good day, my
    dear, good day. Huzza, for Sir John Toddy.   [*Exit.*
3d Freeholder. How weak must Sir John be to be governed by such a
    wretch as Guzzle!

The Sheriff comes to the door, and says,

Sheriff. Gentlemen freeholders, come into court and give your votes, or
    the poll will be closed.
Freeholders. We've all voted.
Sheriff. The poll's closed. Mr. Wou'dbe and Mr. Worthy are elected.
Freeholders without and within. Huzza—huzza! Wou'dbe and Worthy
    for ever, boys, bring 'em on, bring 'em on, Wou'dbe and Wor-
    thy for ever!

Enter Wou'dbe and Worthy, in two chairs, raised aloft by the freeholders.

Freeholders all. Huzza, for Wou'dbe and Worthy—Huzza for
    Wou'dbe and Worthy—huzza, for Wou'dbe and Worthy!—
    (*they traverse the stage, and then set them down.*)
Worthy. Gentlemen, I'm much obliged to you for the signal proof you
    have given me to-day of your regard. You may depend upon
    it; I shall endeavour faithfully to discharge the trust you have
    reposed in me.
Wou'dbe. I have not only, gentlemen, to return you my hearty thanks
    for the favours you have conferred upon me, but I beg leave
    also to thank you for shewing such regard to the merit of my
    friend. You have in that shewn your judgment, and a spirit of
    independence becoming Virginians.
Capt. Paunch. So we have Mr. Wou'dbe, we have done as we ought;
    we have elected the ablest, according to the writ.

Henceforth, let those who pray for wholesome laws,
And all well-wishers to their country's cause,
Like us refuse a coxcomb—choose a man—
Then let our senate blunder if it can.

[*Exit omnes.*

END OF THE CANDIDATES.

THE PATRIOTS

A COMEDY

IN FIVE ACTS

THE CHARACTERS ARE,

Meanwell *Trueman,*	Two gentlemen of fortune accused of toryism.
Col. Simple.	
1. *Thunderbolt,* 2. *Squib,* 3. *Col. Strut,* 4. *Mr. Summons,* 5. *Brazen,* 6. *Skip,*	Members of the committee.
Stitch,	door-keeper to the committee.
McFlint, McSqueeze and McGripe,	three Scotchmen.
Mr. Tackabout,	a pretended whig, and a real tory.
John Heartfree,	a farmer.
Capt. Flash,	a recruiting officer.
Pickle,	servant to Meanwell.
Trim,	a recruiting serjeant.
Mira,	daughter to Brazen, in love with Trueman.
Isabella,	a female politician.
Melinda,	a country girl.
Margaret Heartfree,	wife to John.
Butler, Cook, Scullion and a Servant to Meanwell.	
Groom to Trueman.	

THE PATRIOTS

ACT I.   SCENE I.

Meanwell and Trueman, meeting.

Meanwell. Mr. Trueman, I am happy to see you. In times like these, of
war and danger, almost every man is suspicious even of his
friend; but with you I may converse with the utmost confidence.

Trueman. My dear Meanwell, I know your heart, and am sorry that any
man can suspect its purity; but our case is much the same.

Meanwell. What? Are you too accused of toryism?

Trueman. I am indeed. Unfortunately, I have some enemies who have
raised the cry against me. And what is worse, I fear the conse-
quences will be serious, and a little uncommon.

Meanwell. How?

Trueman. They will be bad indeed if they cause the loss of the girl I
love. To your friendly bosom I may trust the secrets of my
heart. The lovely Mira, daughter of our old neighbour Brazen
has won my affections. You know her beauteous form; but
that is but an image of her soul, its more charming inhabitant.
I had seen and loved her: her father declared his approbation
of my passion, and encouraged me to proceed. Heaven seemed
to promise me success, and the idol of my soul had with blush-
ing tenderness consented to be my bride. But all our hopes
may probably be blasted by this unfortunate circumstance.

Meanwell. Indeed!

Trueman. It cannot be doubted. Her father is a violent patriot without
knowing the meaning of the word. He understands little or
nothing beyond a dice-box and race-field, but thinks he knows
every thing; and woe be to him that contradicts him! His political notions are a system of perfect anarchy, but he reigns in
his own family with perfect despotism. He is fully resolved
that nobody shall tyrannize over him, but very content to tyrannize over others. I happened in conversation to oppose some
of his doctrines of a state of nature and liberty without re-
straint, and he blazed out immediately like a flash of gunpow-

der. I endeavored to moderate his anger; but as reason and he can never be reconciled, I am afraid my sins will never be forgiven: Besides, I have a bitter enemy and rival in Captain Flash.

Meanwell. Ay, that is the drawcansir of modern times; a fellow who pretends to eat the smoke of a cannon fresh from the mouth, and to kill all the enemies of his country, as Caligula would the Roman people, at one blow. But I believe he's a coward at bottom.

Trueman. So do I. But Old Brazen is persuaded that not even Washington is his parallel. As I pretend not to extravagant valour, the captain thinks me a puny milksop, and judges it very great presumption in me to pretend to the lady he adores. I expect he has assisted the old man's prepossession against me; and, by his assertions, convinced him I am a tory.— But this is certain, the old gentleman declared that I should never enter his doors with his consent again, and moreover has commanded his daughter to think no more of having me for her husband.

Meanwell. What a pity it is that all heads are not capable of receiving the benign influence of the principles of liberty—some are too weak to bear it, and become thoroughly intoxicated. The cause of my country appears as dear to me as to those who most passionately declaim on the subject. The rays of the sun of freedom, which is now rising, have warmed my heart; but I hope my zeal against tyranny will not be shewn by bawling against it, but by serving my country against her enemies; and never may I signalize my attachment to liberty by persecuting innocent men, only because they differ in opinion with me.

Trueman. It seems for this very reason you are not accounted a patriot; but truth will at last prevail, the faithful heart be applauded, and the noisy hypocrite stripped of the mask of patriotism.

Meanwell. I hope so; and therefore truth, plain truth, shall be the only shield I will use against my foes. Men who aim at power without merit, must conceal the meanness of their souls by noisy and passionate speeches in favour of every thing which is the current opinion of the day; but real patriots are mild, and secretly anxious for their country, but modest in expressions of zeal. They are industrious in the public service but claim no glory to themselves.

Trueman. May the armies of America be always led by such as these! Thus will the power of Britain be overthrown, and peace with liberty return.— May men like these conduct our government, and happiness, in the train of independence, will bless the smiling land! But before this can be accomplished many temporary evils must be supported with patience.

Meanwell. Yes, and this under which we now labour among the rest.
But what do you propose to do in the case of your lovely
Mira? You won't give up the pursuit?

Trueman. Give up the pursuit? When I do, may I be hanged as a traitor
to love! But it seems a little difficult at present. I have taken
the liberty to use your servant already in the business. As he
very lately came into this part of the country, and possesses a
very genteel air, I thought he might easily pass for a gentleman with old Brazen. I equip'd him therefore as an officer and
sent him to the house of the old gentleman; and ordered him to
pass himself for a travelling captain, and to wait for an opportunity of delivering a letter to Mira. He executed the commission with fidelity and brought me an answer from her, in
which she communicates to me all that I have told you.

Meanwell. And what do you intend to do?

Trueman. With your permission I'll make use of your servant upon a
second embassy.

Meanwell. By all means; but what do you propose?

Trueman. In the pursuit of honorable love few things are reprehensible.
I shall intreat her to elope with me into a neighbouring government, where Hymen shall make us one.

Meanwell. All fair, in my opinion; as you had her father's licence to
win her affections, you have an undoubted right to her person.

Trueman. I am happy you do not condemn my plan.

Meanwell. I will be of your party, your aid-de-camp in this affair. Your
ambassador shall wait on you immediately. In love and war no
time should be lost.   [*Exeunt.*

SCENE II.

A drawing-room.

Mira alone—Mira sings

The constant dove on yonder spray,
Cooing, tunes a moving lay;
She warbles out a tender note,
And fills with love her little throat.
No anxious doubts annoy her breast;
Her mate, the guardian of her nest,
Her pretty young attends with care,
And frees her mind from ev'ry fear.
So the maid, that's join'd to thee,

My lovely Trueman, blest would be
Thy virtues would attune her breast,
To constant ease, to perfect rest.

Oh, Trueman! Nothing but the fear of losing you, gives me
pain. Possessed of thee, I could join the lark to welcome in the
rosy morn, and sing with Philomel[1] the moon to rest.

SCENE III.

Enter Isabella.

Isabella. How d'ye do Mira? Mercy child, how grave you look? Come,
I'll sing you a catch of the new song, that will inspire you, I'm
sure.

As Colinet and Phoebe sat,
Beneath a poplar grove;
With fondest truth the gentle youth,
Was telling tales of love.

There's a song for you.—

But ah! Is this a time for bliss,
Or themes so soft as these?
While all around, we hear no sound
But war's terrific strain,
The drum commands our arming bands,
And chides each tardy swain.
My love shall crown the youth alone,
Who saves himself and me—

What a noble thought is this, my dear Mira! I am determined
never to marry any man that has not fought a battle.

Mira.   Your swain then must have a hard courtship. But suppose he
should happen to be killed?

---

1   Greek maiden turned into a nightingale to escape the sword of her raper.

Isabella. Why then, I should never marry him, you know. But I am resolved not to love a man who knows nothing of war and Washington. War and Washington! Don't you think those words have a noble sound?

Mira. They have indeed; and I acknowledge the smiles of beauty should reward the man who bravely asserts his country's rights, and meets her enemies in the bloody field; but do you love war for its own sake?

Isabella. Lord, no, but then there's something so clever in fighting and dying for one's country; and the officers look so clever and smart; I declare I never saw an ugly officer in my life.

Mira. Your fancy must be a great beautifier, as many of them are not much indebted to nature for personal charms.

Isabella. Ay, that's because you are not in love with an officer. When you are you'll think as I do.

Mira. Are you in love with one?

Isabella. Ah! Now that's an ill-natured question; I tell you, child, I am in love with nothing but my country. If, indeed, a man should approach me, who would lay his laurels at my feet, who could count his glorious scars gained in the front of victory, I might look upon him.

Mira. I suppose, then, if he wanted an arm, a leg or an eye, it would be all the better; or a great cut over his eye-brow would be a beauty spot.

Isabella. Certainly. Nothing can be more elegant. It appears so martial—so— so—quite the thing.

Mira. Well! I'm afraid my taste will never be quite so grand as your's tho' I hope I love my country as well as you.

Isabella. You love your country! Your sentiments are not refined enough: they are not exalted to the level of patriotism; for my part, I scorn think of any thing else.

Mira. Well, but my dear, don't you think the politicians are capable of settling these matters better than you or me?

Isabella. The politicians! and who are such politicians as the women? We fairly beat the men, it is universally acknowledged. And why may not I have talents that way? Who knows but I may be a general's lady or wife to a member of Congress, some of these days?

Mira. I heartily wish you may; but would it not be better not to lose time in thinking about things so remote, and attend more to those of the present moment?

Isabella. Remote, indeed! Not so very remote, I hope! The times are very busy, and great men very plentiful, and no body can tell what will happen. But, my dear, I can't stay any longer. I sent my servant for the papers, and expect he is come by this time.

So child, I wish you a day, and a good husband soon, tho' you don't aspire to marry a general!   [*Exit.*

SCENE IV.

Mira alone.

Mira. That poor girl's head is turned topsy turvy by the little insignificant animal that dangles about her: she has conversed with him, till she has not only adopted his opinions, but caught his ideas. Oh! Trueman, what a difference!

SCENE V.

Mira and Brazen.

Brazen. What damn'd business employs your thoughts, Mira? You are always in a study.
Mira. My principal study, sir, is to please my father.
Brazen. That's clever, my girl. I'll tell you, Mira, I intend to marry you to my friend the captain.
Mira. What captain, sir? There are so many captains now-a-days, that I might guess a fortnight before I hit upon the man, perhaps.
Brazen. Captain Flash, is the man. He's the man, Mira, a fellow of mettle, spirited to the back-bone. He'll fight for his country: those are the men, girl.
Mira. Has he ever been in a battle, sir?
Brazen. He's in the army, child, that's enough.
Mira. Shou'd I not see him, sir, before I promise to accept him?
Brazen. See him! Yes, and feel him too, for what I care; he's a damn'd fine fellow, a fellow of spirit. If you like him, take him; if not, let him alone. I don't care who you take, so he's no tory; damn all tory's, say I.   [*Exit.*

SCENE VI.

Mira alone.

That was aim'd at Trueman; who will ever be suspected as
long as false patriots and pretenders to heroism have my father's ear. Well, as an obedient daughter; I will endure one
tete-a-tete with this fine fellow he recommends. Mercy on me,
here he comes!

SCENE VII.

To her, Flash singing.

Lift up your heads, ye heroes,
    And swear with proud disdain
The wretch that wou'd enslave us,
    Shall spread his snares in vain.
We'll blast the venal sycophants,
    Who dare our rights betray.
Huzza ! Huzza ! Huzza I Huzza !
    My brave America.

Noble, by God! damn me! Here's the stuff, (*drawing his
sword*) shall make the cowardly dogs skip, we'll let the scoundrels see what Americans can do; ha! Miss, your most humble—do you know that I have a vast propensity to quit the
army for your sake?

Mira.   For shame, sir, what! Desert the service of your country, when
she most stands in need of your assistance?

Flash.   Why really, madam, I should be damnably miss'd. Upon my
soul I don't know what they wou'd do without me.

Mira.   Then by no means quit the service, captain.

Flash.   By God, I think I have served long enough. Others should try
their luck as well as I: for a whole year have I been fighting,
thro' heat and cold, wet and dry, hunger and thirst; poor Flash!
Were you not a heart of oak, a compound of steel and gun-
flints, you cou'd not stand it, by heavens! Here's he that fears
nothing. (*sings.*)

     Shou'd Europe empty all her force,
      We'll meet her in array,
     And shout and fight, and shout and fight,
      My brave America.

Mira. Bravo, captain!
Flash. Mars, I adore thee; Mars, was a fellow of spirit, I'm told, the Flash of his day, I warrant it. By God, I wish the lad was here now, that he and I might have a game at tilts together. (*draws his sword and pushes at the wall.*) Ha, ha; there I had him! I'god, now I cou'd gizzard these English dogs, if I had 'em here.
Mira. Pray, captain, put up your sword, I declare you frighten me.
Flash. Frighten you! 'Sblood, madam, the ladies now-a-days should be all amazons, nothing shou'd please them more than a naked sword: however, to please you, up love (*puts up his sword.*) Entre nous, d'ye see, Miss, I do think you are a devilish fine girl. Your father, ma'am, has given me leave.—
Mira. Fie, captain.
Flash. By my soul, he has.
Mira. For shame, sir, a soldier talk at this rate! Fighting shou'd be your theme, captain.
Flash. Fighting! 'Tis victuals and drink to me. I could breakfast upon fighting, dine and sup upon fighting; but after supper, a fine girl, you know—
Mira. War and love can never go hand in hand. Love enervates the soul, and wou'd make the bravest man upon earth a coward.
Flash. Coward: (*draws his sword*) Coward! Damn the word, how it makes my blood boil.

          (*Mira shrieks, and runs out.*)

SCENE VIII.

Flash, alone.

Coward! Ha! If you had not been a woman, well. (*puts up his sword.*) 'Tis no matter, but I'll be damn'd, if ever I speak to you again.   [*Exit.*

SCENE IX.

Melinda, and Pickle dressed like an officer, crossing the stage, meeting each other.

Melinda. Here am I forced to walk three miles to warp a piece of cloth. Mammy says I was born for a fine lady, but I am sure this does not look like it.

Pickle. (*seeing her*) Ha, a beautiful creature, by my soul! Artless and innocent no doubt. (I'll try my luck with her, by God.) Let me see (*musing*) I'll take her in the old way, I believe; address her in heroics, talk of my honourable intentions, and promise marriage. Come to my assistance, dear cunning, and sweet dissimulation; ye true harbingers of lust and love.—Sweet Miss, your most humble.

Melinda. Miss! Lord, how charming that is.

Pickle. (*aside*) Charming girl! By God, I'm at a loss how to begin.

Melinda. (*looklng at his hat*) What a pretty feather! Are you in the wars, sir?

Pickle. I have served several campaigns, Miss, (*aside*) (under the banners of Venus,) I have been in many engagements.

Melinda. I hope you never got hurt, sir.

Pickle. A trifling scratch or two is all the injury I ever received.

Melinda. Do you intend to continue a soldier?

Pickle. Nothing but a wife shall ever induce me to quit the service.

Melinda. Do you intend to marry, sir?

Pickle. As soon as I can get any one in the humour to have me.

Melinda. Any one would not do, I guess: you'll choose some rich lady, no doubt.

Pickle. No, Miss, riches are not my object; I have a sufficient fortune of my own, thank God; I would marry a woman without a shilling, if she hit my taste, such a sweet angel as yourself.

Melinda. Thank you, sir, for your fleers.

Pickle. As I hope for salvation, I would rather have you (*aside*) (for a time,) than any woman I ever saw.

Melinda. 'Tis not worth your while to make your fun of a poor girl.

Pickle. Fun! Upon my soul I'm in earnest.

Melinda. A gentleman like you wou'd never marry a poor girl, I'm sure.

Pickle. There, Miss, you are mistaken: I had rather marry a poor girl than a rich girl. My reasons are the best in the world: a poor girl wou'd think herself obliged to me, wou'd love me from gratitude, and make me an industrious, frugal, good wife; a rich one would think she obliged me, and would want a thousand things, a fine house, fine servants, fine clothes, a fine equipage, all her requests to be granted, and never to be contradicted in any thing. If I marry a poor girl, I get a wife; if a rich one, I get a mistress.

Melinda. You don't mean what you say.

Pickle. I do upon my soul, my intentions are honourable; your name, my dear.

Melinda. Melinda Heartfree, sir.

Pickle. Well, my dear, it shall be Mrs. Meanwell, if you please.

Melinda. Is your name Meanwell, sir?

Pickle. It is, madam. No doubt you have often heard of me, perhaps seen me before: my name and character will remove any suspicion you may entertain of my integrity and honour, I hope.

Melinda. I have often heard daddy talk of you, sir.

Pickle. What is your father's opinion of me, Miss?

Melinda. He likes you mightily, and so does mammy too; you stood for sister Bibby, when you set up for burgess.

Pickle. True, my dear, I well remember it: and are you the daughter of my old friend Heartfree? Come to my arms, (*embraces her*) my dear girl, I shall be proud to be son-in-law to a man of his worth and goodness.

Melinda. You surely are not in earnest, sir!

Pickle. I am, and to convince you of my sincerity, I would immediately wait upon you home, and communicate my intentions to your friends; but I have some business to-day that prevents me: however, I shall be this way tomorrow; will my dear girl be so kind as to meet me?

Melinda. There is no harm in coming here, sir: I can do it to oblige you; but you will forget me, and every thing you have said to me, before to-morrow.

Pickle. Impossible that I can ever forget that sweet face! (*he kisses her, she seems coy*) Will you meet me here about twelve o'clock, tomorrow? Don't be cruel, my sweet girl; you know I love you: my words, my looks, my actions must discover it.

Melinda. Well, sir, I'll be a fool for once, I'll come.

Pickle. Charming creature, one kiss my love (*kisses her*) 'tis ecstacy by heavens! (*Exit Melinda*) Well! these ignorant girls are the finest game in the world: heave a sigh, look languishingly, and swear a little, the poor things drop their heads into your bosom, and die away as quick as a sensitive plant. Well, Trueman, having plann'd a scheme of amusement for myself, I'll now proceed to the execution of your commands.   [*Exit.*

END OF THE FIRST ACT.

ACT II. SCENE I.

A Court-house.

Trueman and Meanwell.

Trueman. What, is the committee to meet to-day, Meanwell? I hate these little democracies.

Meanwell. Take care, sir, both property and characters lie at the mercy of those tribunals.

Trueman. What weighty business calls their high mightinesses together?

Meanwell. Most of the Caledonians[2] are suspected of disaffection to the American cause, and either from friendship or attachment to their own country, disapprove the public measures: from this cause, our holy inquisition are for the very moderate correction the Jews received in Spain.

Trueman. Banishment, or a renunciation of their error, I suppose.

Meanwell. This may be the cause; at present an oath is to be applied as a mirror to their breasts, which reflecting their private opinions and sentiments, must lay them open to the public eye. This is to be offered as a touch-stone of public virtue, as a trial of faith; and woe be unto those who are found faithless.

Trueman. The ungracious treatment that some Scotchmen have met with, the illiberal reflections cast out against them all, give little hope of their attachment to a country, or to a people, where and with whom they have already tasted the bitter herb of persecution: some there are, who have behaved well, conform'd to the public will, nor given any cause of offence; yet even those have not met with the common offices of civility among us.

Meanwell. Of this character are those who are cited before the committee to-day.

Trueman. Hush, sir, here come two of the guardians of our state.

Enter Col. Strut and Mr. Summons.

Strut. We delegates, Mr. Summons, have a very hard time of it.

---

2 Scotsmen.

Summons. Men of abilities must give themselves up to the service of
      their country.
Strut.   True, sir, the people will exact the services of those they can de-
      pend upon.
Summons. Your wise men, as they call them, cut but a poor figure in
      these times.
Strut.   They are dangerous men: they are always starting doubts and cre-
      ating divisions; divisions are dangerous. United we stand, di-
      vided we fall, is the American motto, you know.
Summons. Very true Colonel, very true. When I became a delegate, I
      was told it was the ready way to some profitable post. I long
      to serve my country.
Trueman. Enter into the army, sir; that is the way to preferment.
Summons. I am a cripple, and can't be a soldier.
Meanwell. Be a colonel of militia then, 'tis a fine post for cripples, for
      they never march, but they have no pay, Mr. Summons: you
      want a post that will bring you something.
Summons. I love my country and wish to serve her, and I wish some
      folks were as true to their country as they ought to be.
Meanwell. And as disinterested too, and then men of real merit would
      be in her service, in lieu of them who get into office to catch a
      few sixpences from her treasury.

Enter Brazen, Thunderbolt, Squib and Skip.

Brazen. How goes it? How goes it? Well, what business do we meet
      upon to-day?
Strut. The Scabbies are to be tried according to the ordinance.
Brazen. Let's duck the scoundrels.
Thunderbolt. Duck em! Let's burn the scoundrels.
Skip. Let's hang them.
Squib. Ay, ay, hang them, that is the best way.

Enter Colonel Simple.

Simple. Gentlemen, your servant.
Brazen. How goes it, old cock?
Simple. Why, praise be to God, thro' mercy, I'm reasonably well, I
      thank you.
Brazen. I understand those gentlemen take part with the Scotch. (*point-*
      ing to Trueman and Meanwell.)
Thunderbolt. It is a common talk.
Squib.   The people don't like it.
Skip.   Some talk very hard of it, I assure you.

Trueman. If to treat the unhappy with kindness be an offence, I shall always be an offending sinner; meanness dwells with oppression, and cowardice with insult.

Meanwell. Justice is the birthright of all, and public virtue is displayed by an impartial distribution of it.

Strut. Wou'd you protect our enemies, gentlemen? Would you ruin your country for the sake of Scotchmen ?

Trueman. Prove them to be enemies, shew that they plot the downfall of my country, and courtesy itself shall revolt against them.

Brazen. There is sufficient proof that nine hundred and ninety-nine out of a thousand of them are our enemies.

Trueman. Some may be enemies, others guiltless. 'Tis ungenerous to arraign this man for the offence of his neighbour; illiberal to traduce all for the transgressions of a few.

Meanwell. Justice would blush at such proceedings. Pity drop a tear at the outrage.

Brazen. Here comes the Scotchmen.

Enter McFlint, McSqueeze, and McGripe

Simple. Gentlemen of the committee, pray take your seats. (*they sit round a table.*) I was requested by Colonel Strut, to summon these men here. (*coughs*) I have a bad cold, tell me, if you please Colonel, what it is about.

Strut. (*rising*) These men, gentlemen, are cited before this committee, agreeable to an ordinance of convention.

McFlint. What is our offence pray?

Strut. The nature of their offence, gentlemen, is, that they are Scotchmen; every Scotchman being an enemy, and these men being Scotchmen, they come under the ordinance which directs an oath to be tendered to all those against whom there is just cause to suspect they are enemies.

Brazen. (*rising*) As these men are Scotchmen, I think there is just cause to suspect that they are our enemies. Let it be put to the committee, Mr. President, whether all Scotchmen are not enemies.

Strut. A good notion, Mr. Brazen, I second it with all my heart.

Thunderbolt. We have some Scotchmen in our army; they are our friends, I hope.

Squib. To be sartin they must be our friends.

Skip. Yes, yes, they are our friends, no doubt.

Brazen. They are excepted of course.

McSqueeze. I wish the country very well; I never did it harm, gentlemen.

McGripe. I've gi'en nae cause to suspect that I am an enemy. The ordinance says, ye must hae just cause. Bring your proof, gentlemen.

Brazen. Proof, sir! We have proof enough. We suspect any Scotchman: suspicion is proof, sir. I move for the question, Mr. President.

Trueman. (*aside to Meanwell*) In the catalogue of sins, I never found it one before to be born on the north of the Tweed.

Meanwell. (*aside to Trueman*) In nature's lowest works, I never saw before such base stupidity.

Strut. The question, Mr. President.

All. The question, the question.

Simple. Is all Scotchmen enemies, gentlemen?

All. Ay, ay.

McFlint. Before you determine so precipitately, gentlemen, I should have been glad to say somewhat in my own defence.

Simple. What is it, my dear sir?

McFlint. I was bred in Scotland, but not born there.

McSqueeze. What, Sandy, do you deny your country mon, tak shame to yoursel, Sandy.

McFlint. It is time to deny, man, when they make it a crime to be born there.

McGripe. I'll lose my life for dear old Scotland before ever I'll blush for it.

Thunderbolt. As Mr. McFlint says he's no Scotchman, we have no right to suspect him more than any other man.

Brazen. As he's no Scotchman, he may be a very good man; I move that he be discharged.

All. Agreed, agreed.

Strut. I rise to move, sir, (coughs) I say, sir, I move that the oath be tender'd to these men, according to the ordinance.

McSqueeze. What oath?

Strut. The test oath, sir; you must swear to be true and faithful to this country.

McSqueeze. I'll take nae oath, the like o' that.

McGripe. I'll no swear allegiance to any man but my king.

Strut. There, gentlemen, you see what they are, they are all so to a man.

Brazen. I move that they be disarmed, as the ordinance directs.

All. Agreed, agreed.

Simple. Well, gentlemen, the business is done; I suppose we may rise.

All. Ay, ay.   [*They rise.*

Enter Mr. Tackabout.

Tackabout. Is the committee up? I'm sorry I was not here a little
　　　sooner. I had an information or two to lay before the commit-
　　　tee.
Brazen. We can sit again, sir; order the committee to sit again, Mr.
　　　President.
Tackabout. Upon second thoughts, we'll decline it for the present: I
　　　have not all the proofs about me; besides a witness I expected
　　　is not here, I find.
Squib. I'll lay he has found out some tory.
Skip. He has got some tory in the wind, depend upon it.
Squib. I declare he is the prettiest spokenest man I ever saw.
Skip. Yes, between you and me, he ought to have been our delegate.
Tackabout. Well, gentlemen, you have trounced those Scotch gentle-
　　　men, I hope.
Brazen. We have.
Tackabout. So, Colonel, you have resigned your commission, I'm told.
　　　(*to Col. Simple.*)
Simple. Yes, my friend; I grow old and infirm: I thought it best to de-
　　　cline in time.
Tackabout. There's some prudence in retreating from danger: the times
　　　are perilous, Colonel.
Simple. Young men, like you, Mr. Tackabout, are the properest persons
　　　for commissions: such old folks as I, are better out of the way.
Tackabout. Out of harm's way, you mean, Colonel.
Simple. I think such men as you ought to step forth: I have often heard
　　　you boast of your courage, Mr. Tackabout; now's the time,
　　　sir—now or never.
Tackabout. Why sir, I have some expectations in England; the rever-
　　　sion of a considerable estate, or—
Brazen. Poh! Damn the estate; let it go.
Tackabout. My ancestors lost an estate by their loyalty; I should not
　　　choose to lose mine by my disloyalty.
Simple. 'Tis a sin to lose an estate any how; that's certain.
Tackabout. A man's patrimony, in my opinion, is a sacred depositum,
　　　especially when an expected title gives lustre to the possession.
Brazen. Damn the title—take a commission: that's better than all the ti-
　　　tles in the world.
Simple. Take my commission, Mr. Tackabout: it is expected you should
　　　do something, indeed it is.
Tackabout. I have done enough already, sir.
Simple. But I observe, you keep out of harm's way, Mr. Tackabout.
Tackabout. Where is the man that has done more than I have? I have
　　　damn'd the ministry, abus'd the king, vilified the parliament,
　　　and curs'd the Scotch. I have raised the people's suspicions
　　　against all moderate men; advised them to spurn at all govern-

ment: I have cried down tories, cried up whigs, extolled Washington as a god, and call'd Howe a very devil. I have exclaimed against all taxes, advised the people to pay no debts; I have promised them success in war, a free trade, an independent dominion. In short, I have inspired them with the true patriotic fire, the spirit of opposition; and yet you say it is expected I should do something.

Simple. There are many to be found, who do all this.

Trueman. (*aside*) And few who do any thing else.

Meanwell. (*aside*) Can this be the person we were in company with the other day, Trueman?

Trueman. (*to Meanwell*) The very same, only Proteus[3] like, he can change from a man to a brute, from a brute to a serpent, or to any thing he pleases.

Tackabout. Trueman, your servant; Meanwell, your's. I beg pardon, I really did not observe you were present.

Trueman. We should not have been offended if you had overlooked us altogether, sir.

Tackabout. Poh. Never mind what I say to these fellows; you know my private sentiments.

Trueman. (*aside to Tackaoout*) As well as they do, I suppose, Mr. Tackabout; but, sir, the man who privately condemns, and publicly approves either men or measures, shews himself a knave, and proves himself a coward.

Tackabout. (*aside to Trueman*) Come, sir, no more, sir, I beg of you; I talk to these fellows always in their own style, to avoid suspicion; nothing else, upon honour, sir.

Trueman. So, sir, you inculcate principles subversive of every public and private virtue; you encourage oppression and spread sedition merely for your own security.

Tackabout. Prudence requires something of this kind.

Trueman. What you call prudence, I call baseness, Mr. Tackabout: however, I leave you to the pleasures of your prudent duplicity— Meanwell, I wait upon you.

Meanwell. I'll attend you, sir.   [*Exit Meanwell. and Trueman.*

Brazen. You and the tories were at cross-questions, I believe, Mr. Tackabout.

Tackabout. It is always the case, sir: I wish to reclaim the fellows, and cannot but repeat a little of my political catechism to them whenever we meet.

---

3 In the *Odyssey,* a sea creature that can change his shape to avoid capture.

Simple. 'Tis a pity such clever men should be enemies to their country.

Strut. They are dangerous men; shew me a clever man, and I'll shew you an enemy; let me advise you to keep a strict eye upon those men. Mr. President.

Brazen. Damn all tories, say I. Come, let us go into the muster-ground.

[*Exit omnes.*

SCENE II.

A muster-field (in the court-yard.)

Flash, Thunderbolt, Soldiers, Mob, &c.

Flash. (*holding a news-paper in his hand*) Ha! Damn me, I thought so; yes, yes, honies, you have got it, nine hundred at a clip. Well done, Washington, by God! We'll trip the rascals, damn me.

Thunderbolt. What's that, captain?

Flash. Great, very great; we have done it at last.

Squib. What have we done, captain?

Flash. Every thing, by God; a noble stroke, old fellow; we have killed and taken nine hundred of the damned infidels.

Thunderbolt. Read it, captain, read it.

Flash. Poh! Damn it, you know I hate reading; can't you believe me? There it is, in black and white.

Thunderbolt. (reads) "A copy of his excellency general Washington's letter to congress, dated, Trenton."

Flash. That's it; damn my buttons, if I would not give a million that I had been there.

Thunderbolt. This is great news, really, captain.

Flash. It will do; but it might have been better, and more complete. Some got off, you see; if I had been there, I'll be damn'd if a single scoundrel should have escaped; and here am I doing nothing, but encouraging a set of poltroons to enter into the service; ever perplexed, vexed, and disappointed—not a breath of applause; not a sprig of laurel for poor Flash, while others are reaping it by handfuls.

Thunderbolt. Never mind, captain, it will be your time, soon.

Flash. Soon! The enemy will be driven to the devil before I shall arrive at the scene of action.

Enter Trim.

Trim.   Noble captain, your servant—we shall soon get our complement of men; there are several fine fellows that intend to list.

Flash. Noble fellows: have you any thing for them to drink.

Trim.   I have the recruiting jugs full to the brim.

Flash. Of what?

Trim.   Peach brandy, the best liquor in the world.

Flash. Produce it, damn me, and give the lads a drink.

Trim.   Never mind me; never mind me, captain, I'll do it. (*sings.*)

> Come on my brave fellows, a fig for our lives,
> We'll fight for our country, our children and wives;
> Determin'd we are to live happy and free,
> Then join honest fellows, in chorus with me.
>
> We'll drink our own liquor—our brandy from peaches;
> A fig for the English—they may buss all our breeches,
> Those bloodsucking, beer-drinking puppies retreat,
> But our peach-brandy fellows can never be beat.

          Where's the spring?

Mob.   We'll shew it you.

Trim.   Come on, my brave fellows.

Mob.   Huzza! For the noble serjeant.   [*Exit shouting.*

Flash. My serjeant has enlisted several fine fellows for me; but persecuted with the wheedling of wives, or the entreaties of parents, I am obligd to discharge the cowards as fast as I get them.

Thunderbolt. You should not let your good-nature prejudice the service, captain.

Flash. Prejudice the service! Damn me, sir, I don't know what you mean.

Thunderbolt. I beg pardon—I only meant to say, you ought not to be too good-natured.

Flash. Damn good nature, sir, I scorn it. If I let a man off, 'tis for his money; he pays for his peeping, honey.

Thunderbolt. That's right; it makes the more bounty-money for others.

Flash. No, no, thank you, none of that, my dear; where are my expenses to come from, do you think?

Thunderbolt. I thought the public allowed for these.

Flash. The public allowance is nothing, if it was not for a little smart-money, and now and then a run of luck, I should absolutely perish.

Thunderbolt. Do you ever play at cards?

Flash. A pretty question, damn me! Why gaming and whoring are the first qualifications of a soldier.

Thunderbolt. What say you to a crack at all-fours, now?

Flash.   Agreed.
Thunderbolt. Let us go into yonder house and set to it like brave fel-
            lows: my lieutenant shall play with you for what you please.
Flash.   Here's he that never flinches.

Enter Trim.

            Well, Trim, what luck?
Trim.   Why, sir I got ten clever fellows to promise me to enlist
            (hickups) do you see me, just as the brandy gave out, they
            kept punctually calling for more grog, I told them, says I,
            (hickups) I am very sorry, says I, the brandy is out. E'god, sir,
            the words were no sooner out of my mouth, (hickups) than
            away they went, every soul of them.
Flash.   I am glad of it, for I may perhaps find another use for the bounty-
            money. Trim meet me at old Brazen's to-night. Come, gentle-
            men.   [*Exeunt.*

SCENE III.

Brazen's house.

Isabella and Mira.

Isabella. Prithee, Mira, lay aside those demure looks; when every crea-
            ture is running mad for joy at the glorious news from the
            northward, here are you like an Egyptian mummy—without
            sense or motion.
Mira.   I have a fit of the horrors, Miss, whenever I hear of a battle.
Isabella. So have I, if it goes against us.
Mira.   Victory is attended with the widow's lamentations and the or-
            phan's tears; I cannot rejoice at any thing that sounds with fu-
            neral dirges or makes joy smile in the face of affliction.
Isabella. Were I a lump of clay or an image of wax, the word victory
            would make me spring into life and sing *Te deum.*
Mira.   The untimely death of a parent, husband, or child, might prevent
            your vivacity, Miss.
Isabella. Was I to be mate a widow by every victory, I verily think I
            should rejoice.
Mira.   Parental and filial tenderness are too nearly allied to our natures,
            connubial bliss too valuable, the sweet affections of sympathy
            and compassion are too much the ornaments of the human

heart to be cast away for the foolish exultations that flow from the vain triumphs of ambition.

Isabella. Ha, ha, ha! Do you imagine that I am such a blockhead as to believe the widow's lamentations, the orphan's tears have any effect upon your spirits, Mira? No, no, I know better.

Mira. What do you know, madam?

Isabella. I know that a poor creature of the masculine gender has as high notions of connubial bliss as your ladyship, that he thinks of the great duties of parental and filial tenderness as you do, and that he esteems all victories horrid, unless they are graced with hymenial triumphs.

Mira. You are extremely pleasant, madam.

Isabella. Positively, Mira, I am surprised at you.

Mira. Surprised at me! For what, pray?

Isabella. Why, child, that you should ever think of being in love with one of those horrid creatures, called tories; Trueman is a shocking fellow.

Mira. Really, Miss, I am as much surprised at you.

Isabella. Why, child?

Mira. That you should ever be simple enough to esteem a silly cox-comb in politics, who puts on the name of patriot, as all cox-combs do their clothes, to be distinguished and to be laughed at.

Isabella. What do you mean, madam?

Mira. My meaning requires no interpretation, ma'am.

Isabella. If you imagine your satirical scoffs have any effect upon me, madam, you are much mistaken. The shafts of envy fall short of their mark when aimed at the well guarded, public pro-tected principles of an honest whig.

Mira. Irony is a harmless weapon when pointed either at folly or mean-ness.

Isabella. You are in your own house, madam.

Mira. Where I shall always be glad to entertain you when you are dis-posed to treat me with decency.

Isabella. How have I transgressed?

Mira. Trueman's merits are above the scandal of the times: yet, Miss, it gives me pain to hear his name mentioned in terms of re-proach.

Isabella. I hate tories so abominably that I cannot, for my soul, think of them with patience: as long, madam, as you persist in your fondness for such animals, I shall refrain my visits, I assure you.

Mira. Do as you please, Miss.

Isabella. Madam, your servant; mercy, that any creature can love a tory!

[*Exit Isabella.*

Mira. So, I have lost one patriotic acquaintance—here comes a male bird of the same species to torment me but I'll avoid it.

[*Exit.*

Enter Flash.

Flash. Damn me, if I am not the most unlucky dog that ever cut the cards. (seeing Mira.) So, honey, are you there? Push off, for I'll be damn'd if I'll have any thing to say to you.

Enter Brazen.

Brazen. How goes it, Captain?

Flash. It goes damn'd hard with me, old fellow; I'm sick.

Brazen. Sick!

Flash. Beat to death, trimmed most damnably; a round hundred— nothing less.

Brazen. What! Lashes?

Flash. Lashes! Damn me, what a thought! No, no, here's the stuff, (*laying his hand upon his sword*) here's the stuff.

Brazen. How beat, then?

Flash. A round hundred, good continental, lost with a militia fellow, a damn'd milksop lieutenant.

Brazen. I'll give you satisfaction.

Flash. Satisfaction, sir!

Brazen. Yes, sir; the satisfaction that all gamesters require, a chance to win your money back.

Flash. You mean to use me ill, sir.

Brazen. No, upon my honour, nothing but a joke.

Flash. If that's all, here's my hand, I'm at you, for twenty dollars a game, if you dare?

Brazen. A match, come on.   [*Exeunt.*

END OF THE SECOND ACT.

ACT III.   SCENE I.

A dressing-room.

Enter Isabella, and sings.

No sounds but drums shall please my ear,
Farewell, soft folly; love, adieu:
No griefs but hero's griefs I'll share
Nor sigh, but Washington, for you.

Isabella. Well, what would I give to hear of another victory! I had a
horrid dream last night: I dream't that I saw the congress running out of Philadelphia, frighted to death; some barefooted,
others bareheaded, that they run into a great crowd, where I
soon saw, as I thought, my dear little colonel, bold as a lion,
calling out, to arms, arms! But I was surprised to see the men
have clubs and sticks, instead of guns; and my dear little colonel with a corn stalk to his side instead of a sword. It was a
horrid dream.

Enter Strut.

Strut.   Your servant, madam.
Isabella. Colonel, I am glad to see you.—Do you ever mind dreams,
Colonel?
Strut.   Pleasant dreams are not amiss, madam.
Isabella. Well, but bad dreams, I mean. I dreamt of you last night.
Strut.   Was that a bad dream, madam?
Isabella. Very bad, I thought the congress were running away, and that
you, without a sword, was at the head of a number of men
without arms.
Strut.   Dreams are illusions; but we have had another battle with the en-
emy, madam.
Isabella. When, where! How, tell me, dear colonel?
Strut.   We attacked them at Prince-Town, and have killed, and taken
prisoners, a prodigious number.
Isabella. Thank God: but is it true?
Strut.   As true as the gospel, ma'am: 'tis in the papers.
Isabella. At Prince-town, did you say? Where's that?
Strut.   Prince-Town, is a town, somewhere about—where general Howe
is encamped.

Isabella. Don't you long to be there, Colonel? Lord! If I was a man, how fond I should be of it!

Strut. If my affairs—

Isabella. Affairs: prithee no more of that: when do you think you will set off?

Strut. It is impossible for me, madam—I have some affairs—

Isabella. Affairs, again! Every thing should give way to the service of your country.

Strut. If I had the constitution of some men—

Isabella. Constitution! Why are you sick? Positively, Colonel, if you persist in making such foolish excuses, I shall hate you.

Strut. Upon my honour, madam.

Isabella. That's in my custody, sir: you pawned it to me long ago, as a pledge for the patriotism and courage I have given you credit for.

Strut. I hope you don't suspect me of wanting either.

Isabella. Why really, I never did, but I most certainly shall unless you go into the army.

Strut. 'Tis not necessary that all patriots should be soldiers.

Isabella. 'Tis necessary that you should be a soldier, tho': for, to be plain with you, colonel, I am determined to be a general's lady or never to marry.

Strut. Positively, madam, the service will kill me.

Isabella. You'll be killed in the service, you mean. That's what you apprehend.

Strut. I could die on the field of battle with pleasure, madam, but,—

Isabella. No but's, Colonel, you must be a soldier, indeed you must.

Strut. Well, madam, if it is your desire—but I've one favour to request of you, first.

Isabella. Any thing: what is it?

Strut. Will you condescend to marry me, before I go?

Isabella. No faith, won't I: the conditions upon which I engaged myself to you were as follows: First, you were to be a delegate, next a colonel, then a general. The material condition remains yet to be complied with, on your part; that performed, perhaps I may have no objection to give you my hand.

Strut. Suppose I should be killed?

Isabella. I should cry a little, I suppose.

Strut. My dear madam, there are soldiers enough without me.

Isabella. You must be a general, or quit your pretensions to me.

Strut. I can apply in a neighbouring state, and be made a brigadier-general, without being a soldier.

Isabella. No, no, you shall fight for your commission: I'll have none of your chimney-corner generals, I assure you.

Strut. Will no excuse do?

Isabella. None, sir, I bid you adieu for the present; unless you set off
            for the army immediately, it shall be for ever.   [*Exit.*
Strut.   The devil take this: I have vapour'd away to a pretty purpose,
            faith! By pretensions to patriotism, I became a delegate; and
            putting on the appearance of a man of courage, I became a
            colonel; all to tickle the vanity of this girl—and now, truly, I
            must expose my life that she may be a general's lady! I can't
            do it: I never thought of fighting in my life. What! Stand and
            be shot at! Indeed, Miss, if these are the terms you are to sur-
            render upon, you may keep your citadel forever, for me: I'm
            for a whole skin, if I do pennance in it, as an old bachelor all
            my days.   [*Exit.*

SCENE II.

A field.

Enter Pickle.

Pickle.   Simple creature! How soon she blushed her consent to every
            thing I proposed? Here she comes, fair as Venus, and as Dian
            chaste.

Enter Melinda.

            My dearest girl. (*kisses her.*)
Melinda. I have turned fool, you see, sir, and done as you desired. If
            you were in earnest in what you said yesterday, I shall always
            be ready to oblige you in any thing.
Pickle.   (*aside*) A pretty forward hint, by God. Why, do you see,
            (*scratching his head*) as to that, my dear, we'll talk it over an-
            other time. I have a few preliminary articles to propose to you,
            which if you agree to, you may name the happy day.
Melinda. I don't understand you, sir.
Pickle.   Why, my dear, I have some preparatory measures to take, re-
            specting my friends, and a previous agreement to make with
            you and them.
Melinda. Speak plain, if you please. I don't understand these fine words.
Pickle.   I should be much to blame, you know, to marry any woman
            without knowing whether she would suit my purpose.
Melinda. As to that matter, you can best judge: you cannot look for
            much breeding from a poor girl like me without any bringing
            up.

Pickle. My dear, that is not my objection. I only wish to examine my commodity before I purchase. (*taking her hand*) I wish to know more of you, my dear.

Melinda. (*pushing him off*) You know as much as you shall know 'till you have a better right than you have at present.

Pickle. My dearest girl, as we are man and wife in the face of heaven, do you see, you should not be so very scrupulous with me.

Melinda. It will be time enough to take such freedoms, sir, when I am your wife.

Pickle. (*aside*) Wife! Mercy on us! (*to her*) The liberties I wish to take, my dear, are licensed freedoms. Love requires something of this kind to keep itself alive. 'Tis as necessary to love as fuel is to fire. If you don't let me toy and play with you a little, by my soul, my love will go out.

Melinda. I can't help it; but you shall take no immodest freedoms with me.

Pickle. Poh! A little harmless play, my dear, is mere pastime, don't be afraid. (*attempts to be rude*)

Melinda. You don't behave like a gentleman, sir. I assure you, tho' I might, perhaps, consent to be your wife, I never will agree to be any thing else.

Pickle. (*aside*) Who the devil would have thought it? (*to her*) My dear, I humbly beg your pardon. The violence of my passion is the cause of these transports. Alas! with what delight would I take you for my bride—but the objections of my friends—

Melinda. What friends?

Pickle. I have some particular friends from whom I have great expectations; and your fortune and family would be with them insuperable objections.

Melinda. As to my fortune, and family, it is out of my power to make either of them better than they are: you had better then give over all thoughts of the match.

Pickle. No: it is impossible. My friends shall not control me. I am resolved upon it, and you shall be mine.

Melinda. But your great expectations, sir.

Pickle. Oh! As to that: I hope, in time they may be reconciled, when they find the marriage is over and cannot be prevented. For this reason I think it would be best not to have a public marriage. I will beg you therefore, to keep the marriage a secret for some time, 'till I can reconcile them to it.

Melinda. When I am your wife, you shall direct me in all things.

Pickle. Well, my dear, my servant will wait upon you at this place, about six in the evening, and will conduct you to a friend's house. I'll be there with a clergyman, and proper witnesses.

Melinda. Well, sir, if you do marry me, I will study night and day to
please you, and to make you happy. In the evening, you say?
Pickle. Yes, my love.
Melinda. 'Till then, I wish you well.
Pickle. Adieu.   [*Exit Melinda.*
Little did I expect this resistance in so artless a creature. I
made as sure of my game, as if I had caught it. However, I'll
entangle my pretty linnet yet, in a net often set by us true
sportsmen for these shy birds. Our butler shall be the parson,
the cook and scullion the witnesses. The butler has a most demure sanctified face, and will make a tolerable good priest.
E'gad, the idea of what is to follow, gives me a palpitation at
the heart already. Well, Trueman, your business: then my own.
                                                    [*Exit.*

SCENE III.

Brazen's house.

Flash and Brazen at a gaming table.

Flash. (*rising in a passion*) Damnation seize me, if you did not pack
the cards.
Brazen. It is a damn'd lie, sir.
Flash. Dare you give a soldier the lie, sir?
Brazen. Yes, I dare, when he tells one.
Flash. Come, old fellow, I don't mean to quarrel with you. (*offers his
hand.*)
Brazen. Pay the money you have lost.
Flash. Don't be hard, old fellow; I've no money but the public's, not a
shilling.
Brazen. Public or private, pay, I say.
Flash. Consider, sir, the service must be injured, if I apply the public
money to any purposes, but those for which I received it.
Brazen. Damn the service: what's the service to me? Pay sir.
Flash. I'll give you my note on demand.
Brazen. Your note! Damn your note, I'll have the money.
Flash. Lord! How I tremble with rage, (*sees Pickle coming*). (*aside*) A
brother officer, by God! A reinforcement. (*to Brazen*) My
note, sir, is as good as any man's note. Damn you, sir, you
have raised my blood. I demand satisfaction. (*draws his
sword.*)

Brazen. Lay down your stickfrog, and I'll give you satisfaction. (*puts himself in the attitude of boxing.*)

Flash. What! You are for fisty cuffs? Oh! no, no, honey, I am no black-guard. Come on, my dear. Here's the stuff, honey.

Enter Pickle.

Pickle. Gentlemen, your servant.

Flash. Your servant, my dear. (*stands in the attitude of fencing.*)

Pickle. What! At points, gentlemen!

Flash. Draw, my dear, for the honour of the profession, draw.—Sir, 'tis a disgrace upon a soldier to have a fist cock'd in his company.

Pickle. Your antagonist has no other weapon. Here's my sword, sir. (*offering his sword to Brazen.*)

Brazen. Sir, I thank you. Now, come on, you scoundrel.

Flash. (*to Pickle*) What! Aid the enemy! Hark'ye, my dear, your name!

Brazen. That's Captain Feather, of the flying camp. (*to Flash*) Come on, sir, I say.

Flash. (*to Brazen*) I have nothing to say to you, sir. (*to Pickle*) Captain, I should be glad to speak with you. Walk out, if you please, sir.

Pickle. The sword, if you please (*Brazen gives the sword*) Come, sir, I'll attend you.

Flash. But upon second thoughts, my dear, I can say, what I have to say, here. You seem from the northward, from your uniform.

Pickle. Perhaps not, sir.

Brazen. (*to Flash*) You are a scoundrel, sir.

Pickle. Do you hear that, Captain?

Flash. (*to Pickle*) Washington has done wonders to the northward, sir.

Brazen. (*to Flash*) You are a damn'd coward, I say.

Flash. (*to Pickle*)Are you from the northward, Captain?

Pickle. I am, sir.

Flash. In what corps? In the service of what state, sir?

Brazen. Damn your impertinence; what right have you to catechise any gentleman in my house? (*kicks Flash out.*)

Flash. I'll be reveng'd, damn me, I'll make you pay for this, honey.

[*Exit.*

Pickle. Can that fellow be an officer?

Brazen. Yes; and, I once thought, a fellow of spirit. But he is too mean to talk about. I thought, Captain, you had taken your departure for the southward yesterday.

Pickle. It was my intention when I left this place, Sir. But hearing of Washington's fresh success, I am now hastening to the scene of action, hoping that I may partake of the glory acquired by

	our noble commander in the frequent rencontres with the enemy.
Brazen.	Noble, Captain! Give me your hand. You are for the place of danger, I find.
Pickle.	Danger and honour are two associates that go hand in hand. We must encounter the one to obtain the other. Honour is the idol I worship; to that I would sacrifice my life and limbs.
Brazen.	What can British mongrels do with such men as these. Thirty thousand of them will be but a breakfast for us.
Pickle.	(*aside*) Rather hard of digestion I should be glad to pay my respects to the ladies, sir, if you please.
Brazen.	By all means. They are all from home except Mira. I'll sent her to you. She'll be glad to see you, I'm sure. [*Exit.*
Pickle.	I make no doubt of it. Now, hat under arm, a low bow, and a most obsequious face.

Enter Mira.

Mira.	So, Mr. Slyboots, are you here again?
Pickle.	At your service, madam, and upon an errand of a similar nature to the last.
Mira.	You have a letter for me, then.
Pickle.	Yes, madam, upon my knees I present it; and in token of the great respect I have for the writer, I must kiss the hand that receives it.
Mira	(*reads*)"On Edgehill—at six in the evening—Meanwell and his trusty squire—your affectionate Trueman." You are the trusty squire, I suppose, and can inform me more fully, perhaps, of Mr. Trueman's intentions, than he has ventured to communicate in his letter.
Pickle.	Yes, madam, I can tell you Mr. Trueman's intentions, I believe.
Mira.	Do, sir.
Pickle.	His intentions are to run away.
Mira.	Run away!
Pickle.	Yes, madam, with a beautiful angel like your ladyship and to marry her as soon as he can get a person legally authorised to perform the ceremony.
Mira.	So the plot is out. Well, Trueman, love sweetly supplicates for worth like thine; I surrender.
Pickle.	(*aside*) What a charming creature!
Mira.	Here, sir, deliver this ring to Mr. Trueman; tell him, what he gave me as a token of his love, I now sent as a token of my fidelity to him.
Pickle.	(aside) What a pretty way these fine women have of winding themselves round a man's heart!

Mira.   Inform him, I will play the obedient mistress that I may sooner learn to act the dutiful wife.

Pickle.   Upon my soul, you say so many fine things I shall forget. Do write.

Mira.   Time will not permit, adieu.   [*Exit.*

Enter Brazen.

Brazen. Well, Captain, did Mira know you again?

Pickle.   Perfectly, sir. Miss and I had some conversation yesterday; she recognized me at once.

Brazen. I did not observe you had a word to say to anybody but my old woman.

Pickle.   A little acquaintance gives the tongue a privilege with people of my profession.

Brazen. Soldiers are seldom at a loss for talk, they say.

Pickle.   Very seldom. (*aside*) I'm at a damnable loss tho' to contrive an excuse for getting away decently.

Brazen. Come, Captain, lay by your sword. You'll stay with me to-night.

Pickle.   Excuse me, good sir, when duty commands, the inclination must obey. I should be happy to stay with you many days, but the honour of a soldier compels me to repair to the scene of action.

Brazen. The honour of a soldier! That's true: Well, noble Captain, success attend you.

Pickle.   I thank you, sir, for your civilities, and am your most obedient servant.   [*Exit.*

Brazen. A decent, well-bred lad, and a fellow of spirit, I warrant. Well, I'll go in pursuit of that cowardly scoundrel and cudgel the rascal, or make him pay me my money.   [*Exit.*

END OF THE THIRD ACT

ACT IV.   SCENE I.

A court-house.

Enter Col. Simple and Mr. Tackabout.

Simple. (*with a newspaper in his hand.*) This is great news, glory to the
    Lord for it. The Lord is on our side, I am taught to believe, for
    we have great success, Mr. Tackabout.
Tackabout. Nothing but the tories can hurt us; nothing else, sir.
Simple. Praise be to God they are vastly scattered.
Tackabout. There are many in this county. I am surprised the commit-
    tee don't handle the fellows. I am determined, unless some-
    thing is done with them, to head a mob myself and burn down
    their houses.
Simple. With the Lord's will, something ought to be done. Indeed, there
    should.
Tackabout. You as president of the committee, should cite the scoun-
    drels. Let them be stigmatized; mark them out, and it's an easy
    matter to set a mob upon their backs that shall drive them to
    the devil.
Simple. Why, sir, we have had several before the committee, already,
    but it has pleased goodness that nothing could be mate appear
    against them.
Tackabout. You have tories in the committee, sir.
Simple. God forbid.
Tackabout. Two of the members dined with a Scotchman the other day.
Simple. Dine with a Scotchman! That was dreadful.
Tackabout. Dreadful, sir, why, they deserve to be hang'd. I was told
    they were in a private room, shut up. The person who told me,
    says he peeped thro' the key-hole and saw them wink to each
    other, and then drink; that they would every now and then
    break out into a horse laugh. He heard them drink damnation
    to all scoundrels—very plain.
Simple. That was meant for somebody, I reckon.
Tackabout. It was intended for the committee, sir.
Simple. Well, sir, the committee is to meet to-day, you know, at your re-
    quest. You'll inform them of all such things, I hope.
Tackabout. I'll do my duty, depend upon it.

Enter Brazen, Strut, Thunderbolt, Squib and Skip.

Thunderbolt. Not pay! I thought the captain was flush of money.
Brazen. He's a damn'd scoundrel.

Enter Flash.

Flash. Mighty well! Very fine! Excellent terms, indeed, if the guardians of their country are to be abused by every fellow!
Simple. What is the matter, my dear, sir?
Flash. You know I dare not accept or give a challenge. It's contrary to
ordinance. My hands are tied up you see; yet truly, I am to be
kicked, cuffed, and trod upon. I'll be damn'd if I would not
give a million that I durst cut that fellow's head off. (*pointing
to Brazen.*)
Simple. Surely, my friends, you have not used the captain ill?
Tackabout. Use a soldier ill! They are our dependance—our support—
our every thing.
Squib. Yes, yes, and we should keep them from all harm.
Skip. No soldier ought to be hurt.
Flash. Gentlemen, I lodge my complaint with you. If soldiers are to be
abused, d'ye see me, because they dare not give a challenge,
and by a man too, damn my soul if ever I pull trigger again.
(*cries.*)
Simple. Gentlemen, we really ought to sit upon this matter. (*They all
huddle round a table.*)
Brazen. That is not a business that comes before the committee, sir.
Tackabout. The committee; sir, begging your pardon, have a right to
take up what business they please; and to give any opinion.
Simple. So I always thought.
Thunderbolt. Except against one of their own body. They have no right
to try one another. A lawyer told me it would be *imperium sub
imperio.*
Simple. Why, as you say, my friend, I don't think that would be right,
nor safe neither, indeed.
Thunderbolt. As Mr. Brazen is a member, we have no business with
any matter than touches him.
All. No, no, by no means.
Simple. Well, gentlemen, as that is your opinion, Mr. Brazen, do take a
seat; I say, gentlemen, as that is your opinion, Captain, we
can't do any thing in it, you see.
Flash. Mighty well! Very fine! So I am to be abused and to have no satisfaction. damnation seize me if I don't.
Brazen. (*rising*) What will you do?

Flash.   'Tis no matter, sit still, if you please, I'm done with you, sir. But I'll be damn'd if I don't—(*Brazen goes towards him.*) I swear the peace, gentlemen, I swear the peace.

Brazen.   You are an infamous coward, sir.

Flash.   Very pretty! Noble doings! If I fight, I am to be broke; if not, to be abused; eh!

Brazen.   Walk out, if you please. (*turns him out.*)

Flash.   Yes, yes, I'll go, sir, but damn me if I don't—   [*Exit.*

Tackabout. Upon my soul, Mr. Brazen, I am surprized at you.

Brazen.   For what, sir?

Tackabout. That gentleman is an officer in the service of the country.

Brazen.   Suppose he is.

Tackabout. Our leading men treat our officers and soldiers with the greatest respect, sir. Whatever they do or say, is overlooked for the good of the service.—They would not have one of them offended for the world, sir: they would not, you may depend upon it.

Brazen.   He is a scoundrel; as such I have treated him: if you have a mind —take up the quarrel.

Tackabout. I take up the quarrel! Damn the fellow, I don't care a farthing about him. No, no, old friend, here's my hand; I would not quarrel with you for a dozen such fellows. Well, Mr. President, are the culprits cited, agreeable to the list I gave you?

Brazen.   (*aside*) This fellow has more smoke than fire in him, I find.

Simple.   I told the doorkeeper to summon them.

Enter Stitch

Mr. Stitch, have you summoned them men as I told you of?

Stitch.   I have summoned four; Mr. Trueman, Mr. Meanwell, the Reverend Mr. Preachwell, and a Scotch pedlar, an't please your honour.

Brazen.   What are they charg'd with?

Simple.   Why, Mr. Tackabout there, gave me a paper, with all their crimes set down in it, but (searching his pockets) I've lost it, I believe, some how or other. Howsomever, I can remember as how that Mr. Meanwell and Mr. Trueman are to be tried for dining with a Scotchman, Mr. Preachwell for eating upon a fast day, and the Scotch pedlar for drinking the king's health.

Brazen.   Well, where are they?

Stitch.   Mr. Meanwell and Mr. Trueman, promised to come. The parson snuff'd up his nose as bad as if he smell'd a stink, I'm sartin, says I, it's not me that has let a —, mentioning the thing itself, ain't like your honour. The words were hardly out of my mouth, before spang he took me with his foot.

Simple. The parson strike!

Stitch. Yes; look, your honour, just here an't please your honour. (*shewing his back side.*)

Simple. Praise be to God, our holy teachers detest fighting.

Stitch. I said so, an't please your honour. You a parson, says I! By jing, he ran at me as vigue-rous as a lion, with a monstratious stick; but durn the heels, thinks I, that lets the body suffer; so off I ran.

Simple. Did he say nothing?

Stitch. He call'd me a dirty fellow, an't like your honour.

Brazen. Where is the pedlar?

Stitch. He got the wind of me, and has made his escape out of the precincts, I believe.

Brazen. You say, Trueman and Meanwell promised to attend?

Stitch. Yes, an't please your honour.

Brazen. Suppose we adjourn, Mr. President, for half an hour, 'till the tories come?

Simple. Agreed. (*The committee rises.*)   [*Exeunt.*

SCENE II.

The Court-house yard.

Enter Trueman and Meanwell, meeting Tackabout.

Trueman. Let us secure our pockets, Meanwell.

Tackabout. Fie! My dear Sir, that is too severe.

Trueman. The viper that gives a wound, then licks it with an envenomed tongue, is not more noxious, more offensive, than the base reptile thou art.

Tackabout. 'Pon honour, gentlemen, I have the greatest veneration for you both.

Meanwell. So talk'd the artful serpent when with shew of zeal and love, he seduced our first parents.

Trueman. It is at your instance, Mr. Tackabout, we are called here: What is our offence?

Tackabout. At my instance! You astonish me: at my instance! I scorn it.

Trueman. If your baseness was not perfectly plebeian, Mr. Tackabout, the exteriors of the gentleman might perhaps keep you concealed, but—

Meanwell. Nature is too true to her bias not to make Mr. Tackabout always appear the complete villain she intended him for.

Brazen, Thunderbolt and Simple crossing the stage.

Brazen. Mr. Tackabout is giving the tories a little more of his political catechism, I expect.

Thunderbolt. Come, Mr. Tackabout, no favour to tories: let's have no pleading off; bring them before the committee.

Simple. Yes, yes, let's have them before us.

Tackabout. I have nothing to say against the gentlemen. I have no charge against them.

Simple. Why, dear me! Did not you have them cited. Did not you give me a paper?

Tackabout. (*aside*) That's lost, thank heaven.

Simple. Did not you give me a paper with their names?

Tackabout. I give you a paper! I might give you a paper and their names might be wrote upon it, but not by me, I assure you. (*aside to Simple*) You should never betray your informers, sir. It will stop all your proceedings. It's a breach of faith and confidence that I little expected, sir.

Simple. Oh! dear mel Mr. Stitch, Mr. Stitch.

Enter Stitch.

Where's the paper I gave you with the names of the men you were to summon.

Stitch. An't please your honour, happening to meet with Mr. Pettifogger, the attorney, I shewed it to him. He told me it was a precept and that I must leave a copy of it at every place I went to, but being a poor hand at writing, tho I have a pretty good larning too, I bethought me as how it would do as well to leave the thing itself, so I gave the paper to that gentleman. (*pointing to Trueman*)

Tackabout. (*aside*) Blown, by heavens!

Stitch. The paper Mr. Tackabout gave me, I lost.

Trueman. Here is the paper he gave me, and in my house this was found. (*aside to Tackabout.*) Do you know this hand-writing?

Tackabout. (*aside*) Hide it, for God's sake, my dear sir. Come this way, and let me talk with you. Gentlemen, I wish to have a little conversation with Mr. Trueman. Will you give me leave?

Thunderbolt. Ay, ay, try what you can do with him. (*the committee retire.*)

Tackabout. Do, my dear sir, be advised. You know I'm a tory; if these fellows find me out, I shall be tore to pieces.

Trueman. To this gentleman (*pointing to Meanwell*) and myself, you profess yourself a tory; with these people you have the merit of being a whig. It's high time, Mr. Tackabout, for you to be shewn in your proper colours; for, under your present disguise, you are a nuisance to all parties.

Enter Thunderbolt, Squib, and Skip, listening.

Tackabout. I am a tory, sir, 'pon honour, sir, I am.
Trueman. Then you are the base villain I always found you to be.

Enter Simple, Brazen, Strut and Summons.

Simple. Come, Mr. Tackabout, these gentlemen were cited at your request. Let's have 'em before us.
Tackabout. I have no charge against them, gentlemen. I have talk'd the matter over with them and am proud to find they are innocent.
Simple. Well, well, what a pity! Is there nobody here that can make any thing appear against them? We shall be laugh'd at if they get off so; indeed we shall my friends.
Trueman. You appear anxious sir, to have us arraign'd. By interrogating us you may be furnished with answers respecting any thing you wish to be inform'd of.
Simple. As that is the case, I shall come to the point at once. Are you tories, gentlemen?
Trueman. Explain what you mean by the word tory, gentlemen.
Simple. Tory! Why surely every body knows what a tory is—a tory is—pray, gentlemen, explain to him what a tory is.
Strut. A tory, sir, is any one who disapproves of men and measures.
Brazen. All suspected persons are call'd tories.
Trueman. If suspicion makes a tory, I may be one; if a disapprobation of men and measures constitutes a tory, I am one; but if a real attachment to the true interests of my country stamps me her friend, then I detest the opprobrious epithet of tory, as much as I do the inflammatory distinction of whig.
Simple. How is that? This gentleman is neither whig nor tory.
Trueman. Neither, sir!—Yes, neither. Whenever the conduct and principles of neither are justifiable, I am neither; as far as the conduct and good principles of either correspond with the duties of a good citizen, I am both.
Simple. Well, really, I don't understand him. Do any of you, gentlemen?
Skip. I understand as how he says he is a tory, or no tory, a whig or no whig, just as the maggot bites.
Simple. How is that?
Skip. Why, mayhap, at this present time of asking, he may be a whig, as we pretend to be. By and by he may be a tory, as occasion offers.

Trueman. I detest the mean subterfuge; this low cunning I leave to your
    sycophant, Mr. Tackabout.

Simple. Mr. Tackabout is no tory, I'm sure.

Trueman. Ask him, sir.

Simple. Well, for the joke's sake, Mr. Tackabout, the tories have a
    mind to turn the tables upon you. They seem to signify as how
    you are a tory.

Tackabout. You are better acquainted with me, sir, than to suspect any
    thing of that, I hope.

Simple. Why, to be sure I am.

Thunderbolt. Mr. Tackabout and the tories seemed very thick a little
    while ago while he was talking.

Skip.   Let me tell, Mr. Thunderbolt.—While he was talking with the to-
    ries just now, Mr. Squib, and I bethought us of listening a bit.

Squib.   Yes, and he purtested it was not owing to him these gentlemen
    were summoned. He signified he was a tory himself.

Skip.   So he did.

Squib.   Fair play is fair play; that gentleman call'd him a villain for it.
    (*pointing to Trueman.*)

Skip.   The truth is the truth. That gentleman is lesser a tory than Mr.
    Tackabout.

Squib.   So he is.

Brazen. (*to Trueman*) Give me your hand; you are an honest fellow:
    every tory is a villain. Henceforth, all malice apart.

Thunderbolt. It seems as how the gentlemen are whigs and Mr. Tack-
    about the tory.

Brazen. They are honest fellows, I find. There's my hand. (*to Mean-
    well*) Gentlemen, I move that they be discharged.

All.   Agreed, agreed.

Simple. What must be done to Mr. Tackabout?

Brazen. Duck him.

Skip.   Tar and feather him.

Thunderbolt. Advertise him.

Meanwell. He should be duck'd, as an incendiary, tarr'd as a nuisance,
    feather'd as a foul traitor, hang'd—

Trueman. And advertis'd as a coward. (*kicks him*) I beg pardon, gentle-
    men, but Mr. Tackabout's errors are so fundamental, that I
    can't help applying a certain specific. (*kicks him out.*)

Simple. Well, really, he is rightly serv'd.

All.   Very right.

Brazen. Let us adjourn, and drive the fellow out of the yard.

All.   Agreed.   [*Exeunt all but Trueman and Brazen.*

Brazen. (*taking Trueman by the hand*) You are an honest fellow, a fel-
    low of spirit.

Trueman. I once esteemed you as a friend, respected you as a father,
Mr. Brazen.

Brazen. Well, well, all malice apart, it shall be so.

Trueman. What, good sir?

Brazen. You shall have her to-night, if you please.

Trueman. I am at a loss for words.

Brazen. Poh! poh! Keep your words to yourself; you are welcome to
her, that's enough; as I find you are no tory, that's enough; I
say. Come, let's mob that rascal of a fellow.   [*Exit.*

Trueman. So in spite of all the malice and censure of the times, I am at
last dubb'd a whig. I am not wiser or better than before. My
political opinions are still the same, my patriotic principles un-
altered: but I have kick'd a tory, it seems: there is a merit in
this which, like charity, hides a multitude of sins. Well, Mira,
I have once more obtained your father's consent to our union,
and lest some suspicion or other should again tickle his brain
with the patriotic itch, I am determin'd to be thine this night.

Enter Pickle, not observing Trueman: sings:

The flocks, the herds, the pretty birds
    Nature alone, obey;
Like them I'll range, like them I'll change,
    As free, as blest as they.

Pickle. What he gave as a token of love, I now sent as a token of my fidelity to him. So much for my lesson. (*looking at the ring*)
Alack! alack! How many poor creatures do these little magic
circles make miserable!

Trueman. What fine soliloquy are you meditating, most noble Captain?

Pickle. Taken up with your business altogether, I assure you.

Trueman. It becomes intricate, I fear, if it puzzles a man of your adroit-
ness.

Pickle. I was studying how to convey to you in the best manner, the
sweetest message that ever came from a fond mistress.

Trueman. A lady's message can lose nothing of it's merit when con-
veyed by so great an adept as you, sir, but I expected a letter—

Pickle. A letter! Lord, sir, never ask a letter from your mistress. 'Tis the
worst way of procuring a tender of the affections in the world.
A woman, when she commits her sentiments to paper, is so
very cautious, so nicely circumspect, lest the warmth that ani-
mates the expressions of love should carry her beyond the
usual prudence of her sex, that the glowing ardor of the pas-
sions gives way to a cold prudish reserve, which I call the
grave of love; tho' some are pleased to call it the nursery of

virtue. However, sir, your mistress assents to all your proposals, and here are my credentials. (*presents the ring.*)

Trueman. I know the token too well to doubt the faith of my dear girl,
or the fidelity with which you have transacted the business en-
trusted to you. Take this as a small acknowledgment. (*offers a
purse.*)

Pickle. I never receive wages for conducting a love-intrigue. These little offices of friendship circulate the affections so sweetly, that
I always find a reward in my own feeling without any adventi-
tious one.

Trueman. (*aside*) The youngster's expressions and sentiments favour
little of the footman, methinks.

Pickle. Have you any farther commands, sir?

Enter Meanwell.

Meanwell. Well, Trueman, you have got your plenipotentiary with you,
I find. The preliminaries are all settled, I suppose; and you
have nothing to do but enter the fortress.

Trueman. I have always had a friend in the citadel—the little traitor,
love: but I have obtained by treaty what I lately thought was
only to be achieved by stratagem.

Meanwell. What? Is the old governor in your interest again?

Trueman. Yes, he assents to the surrender, and the terms of capitulation
are all my own.

Meanwell. I congratulate you with all my soul: when is to be the happy
day?

Trueman. This. I am determined to take the old fellow while he's in the
humour. At six in the evening, I expect our plighted troth will
be mutually exchanged. Even that happy hour will have a
shade upon it unless dispelled by your presence: the old gentleman has been rude to you; can you forgive it?

Meanwell. The interest you have in his affection leaves no room for my
resentment. You may expect me: 'till then, adieu.

[Exeunt Meanwell and Trueman severally.

Pickle. Well, since this affair of Mr. Trueman's is to be settled in the
old hum drum style, I have nothing to do but to bring my
amour to as speedy a conclusion as possible. You to your
Mira, Truemand, and I to my dear Melinda.   [*Exit.*

SCENE III.

A field.

Enter Flash.

Flash.   Poor Flash! To be broke if you fight, to be kick'd if you don't!
(*pulls of his coat.*) Lie there, commission and cowardice together. (*draws his sword*) Now, damn me, come on, ha, hah!
(*pushing at the ground*) How I could fight, if I durst.

Enter Strut, escorting Isabella.

Strut.   Well, ma'am, I have taken a commission, purely to oblige you.
Isabella. Your courage must be tried, indeed it must, Colonel, before I
can consent. Stop. (*seeing Flash*) A man fighting his own
shadow. See, my dear Colonel; now is the time to attack him:
do fight him Colonel; I long of all things in the world to see a
duel.
Flash.   Hah! There I had him. Hah! Again, by God! Through and
through damn me! (Isabella pushes Strut up to him.) Mercy on
me! (*starts back and drops his sword.*)
Isabella. Speak to him, Colonel.
Strut.   (*putting his foot on the sword*) Who are you, sir?
Isabella. But stay, Colonel, let the man have his sword. (*takes up the
sword and gives it to Flash.*)
Strut.   May I take the liberty to enquire your name, sir?
Flash.   My name! Damn me, sir, what right have you to my name?
Isabella. He curses you, Colonel; pick a quarrel with him; do, dear
Colonel.
Strut.   What! Quarrel with a madman? The man is deranged in his mind.
Are you not frantic, sir?
Flash.   Frantic, my name Frantic! damn you, sir, I'll not be nick- named
by any scoundrel living.
Isabella. Scoundrel, now we shall have it, draw, colonel. (*She takes
Strut's hand, and puts it upon the hilt of his sword.*)
Strut.   He did not call me scoundrel, madam. He only said he would not
be nick-named by any scoundrel living. I have not nick-named
him, madam.
Flash.   It is a lie, sir.
Isabella. What say to you to that, colonel?
Strut.   The man is mad, absolutely mad, madam.
Flash.   Blood and fire.

Isabella. (*draws Strut's sword and puts it in his hand*) Now, colonel.

Flash.   A pretty blade, let's see it my dear.

Isabella. Let him feel it, Colonel. Up to him. (*pushes up Strut.*)

Flash.   (*puts up his own sword, and advances to look at that of Strut*)
             With your leave my dear, from France, no doubt. I have heard
             they are all the best polishers in the world.

Strut.   Stand off, sir; what did you mean by calling me a scoundrel?

Flash.   I call you a scoundrel! Upon my soul, my dear, you are disor-
             dered in your mind.

Strut.   This lady says you did, sir.

Flash.   Damn all ladies, say I; they are always making mischief, by set-
             ting honest fellows by the ears.

Strut.   I told you, madam, he did not call me a scoundrel.

Isabella. I heard him give you the lie in plain terms.

Flash.   Don't believe her, my dear. You and I won't quarrel about what
             a woman says; they will tell fibbs, damn'd fibbs, sometimes.

Strut.   You hear, madam; he did not give me the lie.

Isabella. Was there ever such a paltry coward! To put up with such an
             affront, and then stand parleying with a fellow who only apolo-
             gizes for it by abusing his mistress? Give me the sword.
             (*Takes the sword and runs at Flash.*)

Flash.   A man in petticoats, by God! Oh, ho! my dear, I smell a rat. Yes,
             yes, honey, catch Flash if you can. Two to one! Oh! no, no,
             my dear; I'll not be assassinated, by God. (*runs off.*)

Strut.   That last reproach of your's, my dear madam, raised my blood to
             such a pitch—if he had not gone off—damn the fellow, I must
             have kill'd him.

Isabella. Colonel Strut, your most obedient. Henceforth, I disclaim all
             connexions with you. Never dare to speak to me, nor hope
             ever hereafter, to see my face again. This I will take as the tro-
             phy of my victory.   [*Exit with Flash's coat.*

Strut.   Well, I don't know whether I am not better without her. She has
             such a cursed stomach for fighting, she would certainly have
             brought me into some scrape or other, in spite of my teeth.

> Honour's a bubble, fame a sound
>   Not worth a man's pursuing;
> Women at best, are evil's sound,
>   And oft bring men to ruin.

END OF THE FOURTH ACT

ACT V.   SCENE I.

Meanwell's house.

Enter Pickle.

Pickle. My master's servants are a set of honest fellows. The butler
made a few scruples at first, but upon his trying on the canoni-
cal habit and my telling him he would make a charming Meth-
odist preacher, by God, the old fellow kick'd conscience out
of doors and immediately became a new creature—

Enter the butler, in a clergyman's gown.

Sage father, your most humble. A little more gravity, and
you'll top the hypocrite so perfectly that tho' true sanctity may
blush at thee, yet iniquity will own thee her's for ever.
Butler. I don't much like the business you have set me upon, Mr. Pickle.
Pickle. Poh! You shall have a buss of the bride, a reward that would
make lechery kick up the beam, tho' weigh'd against the charity of a bishop. Besides, as my tenure will be of short duration,
I expect you may like her in reversion, a gratuity that a lecher
of the Romish church would lick his chops at with avidity.
Butler. It goes against my conscience, Mr. Pickle.
Pickle. Conscience! Ha, ha, ha, as long as you are in that habit, you
may defy the devil and all his imps. Conscience only serves as
a bugbear to the laity, the clergy are above its trifling fears.
For shame, don't disgrace the cloth, old fellow.—Go take the
cook and scullion with you. You know our master is to be at
Mr. Trueman's wedding to night; we shall not be miss'd.
Butler. It is a sin to deceive a poor innocent girl, Mr. Pickle.
Pickle. Poh! Poh! Curse your canting, come along.
Butler. All the sin must lie upon your head.
Pickle. Well, I don't care, so I have the pleasure somewhere else.
Butler. You must bear me harmless.
Pickle. Yes, yes.
Butler. Well, I must go, then, I suppose.
Pickle. Come on.   [*Exit with the butler.*

Enter Meanwell, with a letter in his hand.

Meanwell. My old friend, Mr. Worthy, writes me that his nephew, George, had arrived from England, about the beginning of our public disturbances; that being too free in discovering his political opinions, he was cited before one of their courts. To avoid the treatment he expected to receive from these guardians of the rights and liberties of their fellow- citizens, he absconded without informing his friends of his route or designs. I am requested to make enquiry after him. We have no asylum with us to which persecuted integrity would fly for shelter. No, no, he is not with us.

Enter Groom.

Groom. Mr. Trueman presents his compliments to your honour: says he is gone off to Mr. Brazen's, and desires you will follow him as soon as possible.

Meanwell. (*looking at his watch*) Six is the hour. Tell your master, I'll be with him at the time appointed.   [*Exit Groom.*
My butler just informed me that an old tenant of mine, formerly one of my best and most faithful domestics, has sent to me very pressingly to call on him on my way to the wedding. He has urgent business with me. I must comply with his request, and not to be too late, I'll prepare immediately for my journey. Who's there?

Enter a servant.

Where's Pickle ?

Servant. An't please your honour, I don't know. But since he turned captain, I suppose as how he's after some of his wild vagaries. I saw him out not long ago with somebody wrap'd up in a gown.

Meanwell. You did! Farther enquiry should be mate into this. Do you think any of the servants can tell whither he is gone?

Servant. They say it is a profound secret, but I thinks, your honour, it can't be after any good.

Meanwell. Don't be too suspicious of a fellow servant, but which of them told you it was a secret?

Servant. The cook, your honour: says he to me, Mr. Pickle is a sly cock, says he, and knows what to do, says he, but I hope your honour won't tell as how I told you.

Meanwell. Get ye gone, and tell the cook to come hither.

[*Exit servant.*

That young man is out of the way at a very improper time, and may probably have some trick in view. He appears to be a faithful and honest, and at the same time the most ingenious and genteel servant, I ever saw; but nevertheless, it is not impossible but he may have a mixture of the rake in his disposition. Let me see, what girl is there hereabouts whom he can have in view? It is not my wish to pry into all the actions of my servants, but no improper conduct must be permitted.

Enter the Cook.

Well, sir, can you give me any account of Mr. Pickle?

Cook. Your honour won't be offended, I hope. I don't wish to raise mischief against a brother servant.

Meanwell. You know my authority, when I choose to exert it on a proper occasion, must not be disputed. I understand that Pickle has gone out with some person muffled up in a cloke, and as secrecy is generally the veil of iniquity, I am confident he has some evil design. If you know any thing of his schemes, I insist upon your faithfully disclosing them to me.

Cook. Why, indeed, your honour, he never told me any thing about it; but I have good reason to believe, and I'll tell your honour all I know about it; for tho' I am a poor sarvant, I hope I may be an honest man. Don't your honour think a sarvant has a soul to be sav'd as well as great folks?

Meanwell. They have indeed, and for that reason should be attentive to their duty. But my time is short, be quick in giving your information.

Cook. Well, your honour must know the butler is gone with Mr. Pickle, and he wants me and John, the scullion, to go too. The butler told me Mr. Pickle was going to be married and we were to be the witnesses.

Meanwell. But if that was all, where was the necessity of secrecy.

Cook. Ah! Your honour ha'n't heard all yet! This marriage, the butler said, is to be all a trick. He is to marry her with your name, and the butler is to be the parson, so that Mr. Pickle will gain his ends without any wedding in reality; the butler said as how he did not approve such doings, and he would endeavour to let you know in time to prevent it.—Howsomdever, as he is gone too, without telling your honour any thing about it, I suppose Mr. Pickle may have overpersuaded him.

Meanwell. Bless me! What a scheme of iniquity! But what girl is this he intends to deceive?

Cook. Melinda Heartfree, sir, the daughter of your honour's old servant John. Ah! He is a good old soul, and dame Heartfree too: they

are so kind and good, every body loves them; and the young
girl, too, is as good a creature, and as pretty as ever a man
might wish to see. Indeed, your honour, I think it would be a
pity to do her any harm.

Meanwell. I applaud your sentiments and wish that many in higher sta-
tions, who delight in betraying innocence and beauty, could
think as justly. To prevent the intended villany no time must
be lost. Pickle and the butler may expect you now. You shall
go with me. I'll not stay to dress for the wedding; when suffering virtue is to be relieved, or innocence protected, the mo-
ments are too precious to be dedicated to ceremony.

[*Exeunt.*

SCENE II.

John Heartfree's house.

Enter John and Margaret Heartfree.

John.   Well, my dear, are you ready to take a walk over to neighbour
Homespun's?

Margaret. Yes: I believe there's nothing more to be done about the
house, and I'll go as I am, plain and simple. You know neighbour Homespun don't stand upon finery.

John.   No, and God forbid he should; for neither he nor I have much of
that to brag of. But where's Milly?

Margaret. Milly had rather stay at home, she says.

John.   Well, let her stay; we can go without her. Come, child.

[*Exeunt.*

Enter Pickle and Butler.

Pickle.   Come, I have enquired, and find the old folks are from home.
Melinda is within and will make her appearance immediately.

Butler. What am I to do?

Pickle.   Be all gravity, sir, and with a demure face and most audible
voice read the ceremony.

Butler. The ceremony! where must I find it?

Pickle.   Here, sir, (*opens the book*) you are to begin here.

Butler. Yes, yes, how much is there of it?

Pickle.   All this. (*shews him.*)

Butler. Why it would take me a month to read all that—

Pickle.   Zounds! Man, can't you read?

Butler. Great D-e-a-r, dear, l-y, ly, dearly, b-e, be. l-o, lo, belo, v-e-d,
          ved, beloved, dearly beloved.
Pickle. Pish! try here.
Butler. Great W-i-l-t, wilt, t-h-o-u, tho', h-a—
Pickle. Hush you clodheaded fool; here comes Melinda.

Enter Melinda.

Pickle. My dearest girl. (*kisses her.*)
Melinda. Lord bless me, how my heart aches!
Pickle. What's the matter, my love?
Melinda I'm so scar'd; you'll pardon my folly, I hope, sir.
Pickle. Yes, my dear, and reward your love; this worthy clergyman—
Melinda. Is that the parson? How my heart aches!
Pickle. He is a learned and sage divine, a true Orthodox minister of the
          church, a man of letters, and hard reading (*aside*, literally
          true!) He has an impediment in his speech.

Enter Meanwell, Cook and Scullion, on one side a little behind.

Cook.   There is the poor girl, as I was telling your honour he intends to
          trick.
Meanwell. Is that the butler in the parson's gown?
Scul.   Yes, sir, but he said he would keep them apart 'till your honour
          came.
Meanwell. (*clapping Pickle on the shoulder*) So, sir, you have dar'd to
          make use of my name, in order to deceive an innocent girl.
Pickle. (*aside*) Blown, by heavens.
Meanwell. When virtue stands upon her guard against the protestations
          of lust and treachery, the professed libertine flies to a new ob-
          ject. 'Tis only the sly hypocrite and accomplish'd villain who
          under the mask of honour makes war upon simplicity and in-
          nocence, by prostituting the sanctity of marriage to the base
          purposes of seduction.
Pickle. (*aside*) I am asham'd to look him in the face.
Meanwell. Young man—I could have pawn'd my life upon your princi-
          ples: I have found in you fidelity, sincerity, and truth, an un-
          derstanding and dispostion far above your rank in life. In your
          breast I once thought virtue might have liv'd in concord with
          the graces. Sorry I am to see a mind such as yours polluted
          and abased by the low cunning of intrigue and the base arts of
          sensuality.
Pickle. How much like a scoundrel must I appear!
Meanwell. (*to Melinda*) It is happy for you, miss, that my other ser-
          vants are men of better principles than your fond lover, here.

Melinda. Bless me! What do I hear? Pray, sir, what is the matter?

Meanwell. My name is Meanwell, child.

Melinda. What is your's, then? (*to Pickle.*)

Pickle.   Pickle.

Melinda. Pickle!

Pickle.   (*aside*) Yes, and a most woeful pickle I am in.

Melinda. What a fool have I been?

Pickle.   Pardon me, good sir; and you, my dear girl, forgive me. Tho'
            your virtue deserves a greater reward, yet, if you will conde-
            scend to marry me, it shall be the future study of my life to
            atone for my base designs upon your unsuspecting love by
            making you a kind and most affectionate husband.

Melinda. Your friends will object to your marriage unless you get a
            woman of family and fortune, perhaps.

Pickle.   My principal friend is here present: If he consents, and you are
            willing, there can be no other objection to our union.

Meanwell. The generous tender you make of your hand and affections
            to this poor injur'd innocent gives me hopes that you have not
            travelled far in the road of vice. Her example will, I hope, re-
            call you to the paths of virtue. If she is willing, I not only con-
            sent to your union, but will present you with a sufficient sum
            to begin the world with.

Pickle.   (*aside*) Noble fellow. (*to her*) Well, my dear Melinda, you hear
            this; can you forgive me?

Melinda. It was your person I lov'd, not your fortune. Your person is
            still the same, I must still love.

Pickle.   Here's my hand.

Melinda. With mine take my heart.

Butler.   Well, as all matters are settled, I may read the ceremony, I sup-
            pose. I can read much better now, Mr. Pickle.

Meanwell. Come, sir, be merciful, when virtue rides triumphant on the
            smooth surface of our affections, you should never ruffle the
            fair prospect by stirring the passions.

Melinda. Instead of a fine lady, I must be poor Melinda still; and in-
            stead of the master I've got the man. (*taking Pickle by the
            hand, sings.*)

> But come, my Pickle, to my arms,
> With all thy love attracting charms,
> And free my mind from all alarms.
> No sordid views, in thirst of gain,
> No hopes of riches giving pain,
> Shall e'er disturb my simple brain.
> My loom shall tell, my wheel declare
> That no domestic feuds, or war,

Shall drive my Pickle from my care.
I'll spin his coat, I'll knit his hose,
With white the legs, with blue the toes,
And keep him heat where'er he goes.

Pickle. My dear, Melinda, it is with pleasure I shall now discover to you my real name and character.—After the proofs I've had of your virtue and disinterested love, I can no longer hesitate in making you mistress of a fortune equal to that I falsely pretended to be master of.

Meanwell. What is this I hear?

Melinda. More wonders still!

Pickle. That gentleman (*pointing to Meanwell*) will be able to inform you that there are few families in this western hemisphere superior to mine, either in estate or other circumstances. By the death of a tender and careful father, I am possessed of an ample fortune.

Meanwell. (*aside*) My suspicions increase every moment.

Pickle. The phrenzy of the times, and an unhappy attachment to sentiments and opinions inculcated into me from my early youth, reduced me to the necessity of abandoning both friends and fortune for a time, and to seek an asylum under the roof of a man held high in the esteem of my poor deceascd father and revered by all his dependants.

Meanwell. (*shewing a letter*) Do you know this hand writing?

Pickle. It is my good uncle's, or I'm much deceiv'd.

Meanwell. Come to my arms, my dear George; son to the companion of my youth, the fond associate of my riper years. He will always live in my remembrance, and to thee I will pay the debt of love I owed him.

Pickle. All no more to what I have received, lest you oppress me with accumulated kindness.

Meanwell. My dear George why did you come to me in the character of a footman? You know the interest you had in my affections which entitled you to a station far above the lowly homage paid to a master, or that pliant duty service too often requires.

Pickle. Hearing that you were a suspected person as well as myself, and apprehending I might be held out to public odium, as the phrase is, I fear'd if I announc'd myself to you, you might be induced to do something in my behalf, which would render you still more obnoxious than you are at present.

Meanwell. Is it not sufficient that public virtue sometimes yields to the torrent of political enthusiasm, but are the social virtues to be confined within the narrow circle of self-preservation or hid under the disguise of time-serving civility?

Enter John and Margaret Heartfree.

My old friend, I am glad to see you. (*shaking John by the hand*) Madam, your servant. (*to Margaret.*)

John.   I am proud to see your honour. Heaven's bounty be prais'd, your honour bears a good face yet.

Margaret. And a good heart too, I hope (*curtseying.*)

Meanwell. Thank you, my good old lady; you wish me a boon far above the treasures of the world.

John.   Well, but Milly, how comes it that the gentlemen are all standing, child? Come, sir, take a seat; nobody welcomer, your honour knows.

Meanwell. I thank you John, I had rather stand. (*pulling out his watch*) I have no time upon my hands, I find. Well, what business have you with me, John?

John.   Business! bless your honour, I am proud to see you: it always does me good, whenever your honour comes a near me.

Butler.   (*to Meanwell*) It was a feign'd story of mine to bring you here, sir.

Meanwell. Is that it? I'll say no more about it, then. So, John? you were near having a wedding in your house today.

John.   I don't know how that could be, unless Milly would have wedded one of the bed-posts. There has not been a soul here, that I remember, off and on these two months and better.

Margaret. Except the mad Captain; he was here anon.

Meanwell. What do you think of this gentleman?

John.   I don't recollect that ever I saw him before.

Meanwell. This is a young gentleman of fortune, the son of an old friend of mine. His name is Worthy, and would be happy to marry your daughter, if you will grant your consent.

John.   Your honour must be joking now.

Meanwell. Indeed I am not; certain circumstances compelled him, for a while, to pass himself on the world for my servant by the name of Pickle; but his passion for Melinda has induced him to discover his real name and family.

John.   I cannot doubt your honour's word. But how came he acquainted with Milly?

Pickle.   Love, tho' blind, by instinct finds his way. I confess, with shame, that when I first saw this beauteous maid, I was tempted to entertain dishonourable designs upon her, but I found her pure as spotless snows, and firm as adamant against all improper proposals, tho' soft as wax to the impressions of tenderness. I have always wished to find a maiden who could love me for myself alone; in this artless fair I have found one who when my base attempt to impose upon her by a pretended marriage, was discover'd, mov'd my affection, forgave it all, and deign'd to receive the repentant sinner, tho' seemingly poor and humble. To her then, I bow, and she, if you object not, shall be the partner of my future life.

John. All this is new to me; but the gentleman is welcome to Milly, with all my heart. However, as it is come to this, another secret must be explained, for that girl is no more my daughter than I am a governor.

All. How?

John. No, your honour, she is of a much better family than I shall ever boast: she is nearly related to your honour.

Meanwell. To me!

John. Yes, your honour; but a short story will make all clear. You remember you had a sister once who is now dead?

Meanwell. Yes, one whom I have always remembered with lively regret. She marri'd unhappily.

John. There, your honour, was the beginning of all the mischief. You know Mr. Spendall, her husband was a very extravagant man. He liv'd at a great rate, and gam'd and horse-raced it very much so that he soon brought himself to ruin. But that was not all, for, besides all this, he treated the lady, his wife, very ill, indeed. She had brought him a fine fortune, and he had spent it: so he thought her heart always upbraided him for it, and that made him worse, but Lord help the poor lady, she was so sweet and kind hearted, she bore no malice to any body.

Meanwell. (*weeping*) Your tale touches me too tenderly.

John. No wonder it should, your honour, but as I was about to say, the poor lady you know had a child, which was generally supposed to have died when it was two months old. Her husband was at that time gone upon a long journey which he took indeed to keep out of the way of his creditors, and the report was spread to deceive him, and a pretended funeral was had.

Meanwell. I remember it, and I attended on the occasion, but I did not examine the coffin.

John. Neither did any body else: but the poor lady had brought the child to me. I shall never forget her looks. It was not long before she died. John, says she, I know I shall shortly die, my heart is broken, and I am going to a better world than this. My only tie to earth is this tender infant: may she never feel her mother's sorrow! This infant I cannot leave in the house of a man who has forgotten all the feelings of a husband, who would educate her in vice, and perhaps leave her to beggary. I can preserve her from the pollution of bad example only by removing her from him. With you she will be plain and virtuous. When I am dead, and my husband is no more, who I know when alive will never permit her to reside with him, convey her to my brother if he shall then be living. I know his generous soul: he will be indeed a father to her: as a proof of her birth, present him with this picture of his wretched sister, which he gave her himself. Here it is, an't please your honour. (*shews a miniature picture.*)

Meanwell. It is indeed, the same.

John.   Tell him, she said, that is the picture of his once dear Caroline, tell him it is the only valuable pledge of affection I had to leave him. She went away weeping so bitterly that every time I think on't.—(*wiping his eyes.*)

Meanwell. (*taking Melinda in his arms*) My dearest girl—say, John, is this my poor sister's child?

John.   I'll be sworn.

Meanwell. How can I doubt it? These eyes tempered with sweetness, these looks of mildness declare the fountain from whence they take their origin. (*embracing her.*)

Margaret. Blessing upon her; she is as good a child, tho I say it, and had the bringing of her up, as ever suck'd it's mother milk.

Meanwell. (*to Pickle*) Come hither, George; the generous tender you have made of your person and fortune to this girl, shall be amply rewarded. Take her, not as poor Melinda, but as my niece, and with her a fortune equal to your wishes.

Pickle.   Her merit is a sufficient dowry; her beauty would tempt the miser to forget his gold and even think of happiness.

Melinda. (*runs to John and Margaret embracing them alternately*) My dear father, my dear mother, how comes it that I am not your daughter? I am, I must be, indeed I must.

Meanwell. Their kindness, my dear, well deserves a filial attachment. It shall be my part to acquit you, in some measure, of the obligations you are under to them, by something more substantial than words.

John.   Come, Milly, place your mind upon your uncle; he is worth a dozen such fathers as I am, child.

Melinda. My uncle, I shall respect, no doubt, shall love; but must I forget my poor good old father and mother, who have fed me, rais'd me, cherish'd and loved me so long? I could as soon forget my victuals and drink, as forget those to whose kindness I have so long been indebted for both.

Meanwell. When gratitude displays itself, it is with a meridian brightness, that almost casts a shade over the sister virtues.—But, John, why did you keep this matter a secret from me?

John.   Your honour married, you know, soon after my young mistress went away. Ever since your poor lady died childless, I have been thinking of telling your honour, but some how or other, my heart has always misgiven me 'till now.

Meanwell. Well, my dear niece, I must redeem the time you have been lost to my affections by redoubled tenderness for the time to come. Your old friend, Mr. Trueman, is to be married this evening. John, will you and the old lady go with us to the wedding?

John. I am always ready to obey your honour's commands. Milly, you must go behind your spouse, I suppose. The old woman and I can walk.

Meanwell. By no means, take my servant's horses. They can wait here 'till our return.

John. Well, well, your honour's will is my pleasure.

Meanwell. Come, let's away.

[*Exeunt.*

SCENE III.

Brazen's house.

Enter Mira.

Mira. I wish love and duty could always go hand in hand, but the little tyrant will be obey'd, even when all the virtues oppose him. What can poor Duty do when sole competitor against so formidable a rival. She must submit, I suppose. (*sings.*)

Hail, Cupid, god of love, to thee
Henceforth I'll bend the suppliant knee;
Hymen, to thee my bliss I'll owe,
And fearless to thine altar go.

I have long given up to filial piety all the little gratifications and amusements so ardently pursued by the gay and giddy of my years, but I can never resign to an arbitrary injunction, proceeding from mere caprice, the fair prospect I have of a happy establishment thro' life.

Enter Trueman.

My dear Trueman, how came you here? Surely my eyes deceive me; it can't be you.

Trueman. My love, my life, my every hope! (*embracing her.*)

Mira. For God's sake, my dear sir—I expect my father, every moment.

Trueman. Let him come. (*kissing her*) This prattling talk of love, would make the angry tenants of the forest club their songs, and all the winged race chirp to the melody.—(*kissing again.*)

Mira. If he should come, and find you here!

Trueman. Lay aside your fears; your father has again consented to our union. What his inducements are, 'tis needless to relate at present. Let it suffice, that here I am by his permission.

Mira. Is it possible?

Trueman. True as my love, doubtless as your fidelity.

Enter Brazen.

Brazen. So, so, give these young dogs a scent of the scut and away they fly, regardless of whip or horn. Well, I am glad to see you, sir; Mira, how goes it, child.

Trueman. (*taking Mira by the hand*) You set before you, two persons, long united by the ties of love, now waiting only for the solemn, sacred, service the rites of honour call for.

Brazen. I hate your high flown speeches, Mr. Trueman.

Mira. My dear father, at your request, I was induced to accept a tender of this gentleman's affections.

Brazen. You begin upon your high ropes. Hush, take him, that's enough, (*joining their hands*) here, now, you are both satisfied, I hope.

Mira. (*kneeling*) Accept my thanks.

Brazen. Kneel to your maker, child, not to me; get up. You may have him, I say, that's enough.

Enter Meanwell, Pickle, Melinda, John, and Margaret Heartfree.

Trueman. My dear Meanwell, (*presenting him to Brazen*) Mr. Meanwell, sir.

Brazen. Poh! I know him well enough. I have eyed him many a time, damn'd sharp, too, you may depend. However, as he is no tory, I have nothing more to say. Here's my hand. I'm glad to see you, sir. Who have you with you?

Meanwell. Mr. Worthy, sir. (*introducing Pickle.*)

Brazen. Worthy! No tricks upon travellers. I am glad to see you, Captain.

Meanwell. Miss Spendall. (*introducing Melinda.*)

Brazen. Milly Heartfree, as I live! You have a mind to be funny, sir, but you can't cheat me in my neighbour's children, neither. (*to John and Margaret.*) How goes it, neighbours? I am glad to see you. Come, take seats. I'll go, and have a rouzing fire in the great room. (*sees Trueman kissing Mira*) How they bill like two pigeons! The parson will be here presently. He'll set you to kissing, with a vengeance.   [*Exit.*

Trueman. (*to Meanwell*) You are quite funny with the old gentleman.

Meanwell. I never was more serious in my life. This, sir, is George Worthy, of Maryland, nephew to our good friend and acquaintance, Charles Worthy, Esq; and this—can you believe it?—is my niece, my dear sister's daughter.

Trueman. I am astonished.

Mira. I never was more so in my life.

Meanwell. Let it suffice for the present to inform you they are affianced to each other. The circumstances which have led to a discovery of their rank in life and the generous proofs each has received from the other of a disinterested affection, I will give you in full at a more convenient season. Their wedding is to follow your's. Will my Trueman and his lovely bride favour us with their company?

Trueman. Doubtless.

Mira. With pleasure, sir.

Enter Brazen.

Brazen. Come, adjourn into the next room, if you please. Old Thump-the- cushion is arrived already.

[*Exeunt omnes.*

END OF THE PATRIOTS

For a free descriptive catalog, write to:

Geodesics Publications, Inc.
848 N. Rainbow Blvd. #2269
Las Vegas, Nevada 89107

Made in the USA
Middletown, DE
25 November 2020